5/09

It's Only Temporary

Written and illustrated by

SALLY WARNER

VIKING

VIKING
Published by Penguin Group
Penguin Young Readers Group, 345 Hudson Street, New York, New York 10014, U.S.A.
Penguin Group (Canada), 90 Eglinton Avenue East, Suite 700, Toronto,
Ontario, Canada M4P 2Y3 (a division of Pearson Penguin Canada Inc.)
Penguin Books Ltd, 80 Strand, London WC2R 0RL, England
Penguin Ireland, 25 St Stephen's Green, Dublin 2, Ireland (a division of Penguin Books Ltd)
Penguin Group (Australia), 250 Camberwell Road, Camberwell, Victoria 3124,
Australia (a division of Pearson Australia Group Pty Ltd)
Penguin Books India Pvt Ltd, 11 Community Centre,
Panchsheel Park, New Delhi – 110 017, India
Penguin Group (NZ), 67 Apollo Drive, Rosedale, North Shore 0632,
New Zealand (a division of Pearson New Zealand Ltd.)
Penguin Books (South Africa) (Pty) Ltd, 24 Sturdee Avenue,
Rosebank, Johannesburg 2196, South Africa

Penguin Books Ltd, Registered Offices: 80 Strand, London WC2R 0RL, England

First published in 2008 by Viking, a division of Penguin Young Readers Group

1 3 5 7 9 10 8 6 4 2

LIBRARY OF CONGRESS CATALOGING-IN-PUBLICATION DATA
Warner, Sally.
It's only temporary / written and illustrated by Sally Warner.
p. cm.
Summary: When Skye's older brother comes home after a devastating accident, she moves
from Albuquerque, New Mexico, to California to live with her grandmother and attend middle
school, where she somewhat reluctantly makes new friends, learns to stand up for herself and
those she cares about, and begins to craft a new relationship with her changed brother.
ISBN 978-0-670-06111-2 (hardcover)
[1. Brothers and sisters—Fiction. 2. Friendship—Fiction. 3. Bullying—Fiction.
4. Brain damage—Fiction. 5. Grandmothers—Fiction. 6. Middle schools—Fiction.
7. Schools—Fiction. 8. Sierra Madre (Calif.)—Fiction. 9. Albuquerque (N.M.)—Fiction.]
I. Title. II. Title: It is only temporary.
PZ7.W24644It 2008
[Fic]—dc22
2007038220

Manufactured in China   Set in Excelsior

To "The Steps": Eli Siems, Will and Julia Bosley,

and Lucy and Noah Parsons

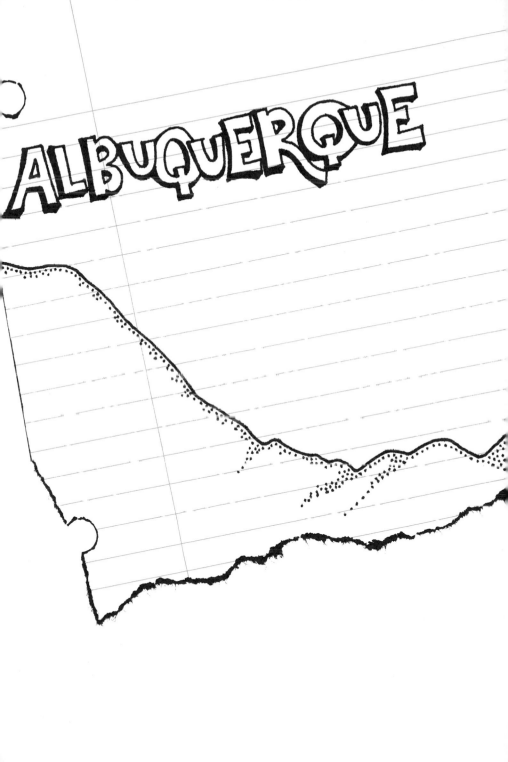

1

Worst Field Trip Ever

A nd now that he was so messed up, she couldn't hate her impossible big brother even a little, twelve-year-old Skye McPhee thought moodily as she stared out of the car's rear window. She and her parents were driving west on Interstate 40 toward the spot where Scott had totaled their other car nearly four months earlier, only three days after getting his license.

This had to be the worst field trip ever, Skye told herself. But her mom was determined that they should visit the accident site before bringing Scott home from rehab for a trial visit—and for the holiday. She thought it would help them count their blessings.

It was the third of July, and blazing hot outside their air-conditioned car. Skye opened her sketchbook and reached into her tote bag for a drawing pen.

At least Scott hadn't died, Skye thought as they passed a shabby roadside memorial probably built to honor some unluckier reckless kid—because in New Mexico, people very often placed a little white cross by the side of the road when someone died in a car accident. Then they decorated the cross with plastic flowers, which was a good reason all

by itself not to die like that, Skye told herself, shuddering, because—plastic flowers! And then white grocery bags blew across the desert and got tangled up like shredded ghosts in the faded, grimy flowers, and the whole thing just got sadder and sadder.

"We've already passed Laguna Pueblo," Skye's mother told her husband, sounding as if there were a rubber band wrapped tight around her vocal cords. "We must be pretty close. Pull over, Daniel."

"I'm trying, if the guy behind me would just give me a break and ease up a little," Skye's father said, his voice equally strained.

"Well, signal," her mother said.

But her nervous dad's right turn signal had been on

View from the backseat
(I can't help it! I draw EVERYTHING!!)

for at least a mile, Skye thought, gritting her teeth and closing her eyes as her father's car swerved suddenly to the right and rolled to a stop at the side of the busy highway. A truck's horn blared as the stream of vehicles that had built up behind them whooshed by.

"There," her father said, his voice unsteady. "Are you happy?"

"Deliriously," Skye's mother told him. "Deliriously."

"We're here, so let's take a look," Skye said, hoping they wouldn't start fighting again. Not here, not now.

"Don't get out, Skye," her mother told her, sounding scared. "It's not safe."

"I know that," Skye mumbled. "This was a dumb idea," she said, growing bolder. "We can't see—"

"It's over there," her father said quietly, pointing. "It's just over there." He looked down and adjusted an air-conditioning vent toward his face.

Her dad had been out here before, Skye reminded herself as she tried to see where her family's other car had tumbled end-over-end that cold March night. Today, a cloudless blue sky wheeled overhead, and the gray-green scramble of nearly flat desert shimmered and stretched before her eyes, an expanse punctuated only by dark scrubby bushes and a billboard.

The only weird things about this landscape were the black skid marks on the pavement—lots of skid marks, Skye noted, although the highway was as straight as could be along this stretch—and some strange, deep-yellow scrapes in the earth that headed off into the desert as if leading to a place Skye didn't want to go.

"But—there's nothing here," her mother said, her voice as small as a girl's. "I don't understand. What did Scotty hit?"

"Nothing," Skye's father said. "He was going pretty fast."

He'd probably been reaching for a CD, Skye thought, frowning—or, more likely, flipping off another driver. Scott was famous for his bad temper, after all. Maybe he'd been forced off the road, she thought suddenly; they'd never know.

⚘ SCOTT'S ACCIDENT ⚘

1. Okay, anyone can make a mistake.
2. But when you make a mistake with a CAR, that's serious.
3. And anyway, Scott's accident was probably his own ≈STUPID FAULT.≈
4. So does that mean we don't have to take care of him?
5. No.
6. But I can still be mad at him.

Scott sure couldn't tell them. He didn't remember a thing about that night.

"We'd better get going. We're supposed to be at rehab by two," Skye's father said. "If you really think bringing him home is a good idea."

"The insurance company thinks it's a good idea," Skye's mother reminded him dryly. "And I'm pretty sure we can manage it. Sooner or later I want my baby to come home, Danny, so it might as well be now."

"We can give it a try, at least," Skye's father said, looking over his shoulder for a break in the traffic as his left turn signal ticked. "We can turn around on that reservation road."

The imposing turnoff to the road that led south to the ancient and isolated Acoma Pueblo looked as if it were headed toward a big city, rather than a distant hilltop. Most of the inhabitants of the reservation now seemed to live in the satellite dish–studded houses and trailers scattered sparsely along this reservation road, however, and Skye sketched, wondering what their lives were like.

"Turn the car around, Daniel," Skye's mother said. "Or we're going to be late."

"There's a wide place just past that little cemetery, if I recall correctly," Skye's father said as he rounded a corner. "What the—" His exclamation faded as he made his way past an unexpected lineup of parked cars and pickups parked on both sides of the narrow dusty road. "It's a funeral," he announced, his voice flat.

Skye's mother gasped—which just about said it all, in Skye's opinion.

She couldn't help but look, however.

In spite of the intense midday heat, people of all ages were streaming quietly through a wrought-iron gate and into the barren cemetery, which was surrounded by a low wire fence. The people were neatly dressed in dark jeans and ironed shirts, Skye observed, and at the head of each carefully tended grave was a small wood cross that had been painted white.

It's Only Temporary

A woman with shining black hair flowing
loose to her waist stood near the gate. She was
holding a black-and-white bowl, and many of the
people entering the cemetery slipped money into the
bowl as they passed, probably to help pay for the funeral,
Skye guessed.

They ignored her family's car.

"Don't stare, honey," Skye's father said, catching her
eye in the rearview mirror. "This is a private moment for
them."

"I know, Daddy," Skye murmured, looking away. But
she could still picture every detail of the scene.

It was nice here, she thought, her spirits unexpectedly
lifting, and it was peaceful, and perfectly perfect in every
perfect way: the sky, the heat, the little white crosses, the
beautiful bowl, the quiet people.

This was the way the end of life was supposed to be.

And this was probably how it should have been—for
Scott.

Skye couldn't help but think that.

2

"The Loonies"

"Late," Scott exclaimed angrily from his wheelchair as Skye and her parents walked into his wide-doored room. "Late, late!"

"I'm sorry, sweetie," Mrs. McPhee said, hurrying to his side. "We wanted everything to be just perfect for you at home, that's what happened."

Let the lies begin, Skye thought grimly, forcing herself to look at what was basically a brand-new brother. He was planted in his chair like a TV judge, and he glared at his family as if his condition was all their fault.

Scott's TBI—his "traumatic brain injury"—was the worst result of his accident, Skye had been told, though you couldn't tell that just by looking at him. But the TBI was the injury that would take the longest time to heal—if it ever fully did.

As for the rest of him, Scott's ankle was still in a cast, as was his left arm. The scar on his right cheek had faded a little, Skye was relieved to see, but her brother still looked like Frankenstein's monster. Maybe it was his expression, Skye thought, but he didn't truly seem like her brother anymore. Not that he had for a long, long time.

They used to be friends. But then, when he was twelve and she was about eight, Scott had started messing up: talking back to their mom and dad, slamming doors, "forgetting" to do both chores and homework assignments. He'd concentrated all his attention on his small circle of friends, friends who'd grown sketchier as the years passed—except for Stacie, his almost-girlfriend, who seemed nice.

Scott McPhee

Recently, Scott had started lying in a big way—to everyone—and cutting class, and, later, sneaking out at night.

Then there was the accident, and Scott was different now. His quirky expression and blazing blue eyes were the same as before, but some important part of him seemed to have been left behind in the desert that cold March night.

"Stoppit," Scott snapped, looking at Skye. "Quit looking!"

"I didn't do anything," Skye mumbled, staring down at the shiny floor again.

"Did they round up everything you'll need for the holiday, son?" Mr. McPhee asked in his most bustling, take-charge tone. "Are you all packed?"

"Uh," Scott grunted, looking away. "I hate it here!" he shouted suddenly, pounding the arm of his wheelchair so hard that Skye jumped.

"The Loonies," Scott had painfully managed to call Las Lunas Rehabilitation Unit during Skye's one and only other visit a few weeks earlier, and that small joke was the only thing so far that had given her anything like hope for him.

But now . . .

"We know you hate it here, darling," Mrs. McPhee murmured, trying to calm him down. "But I don't see your suitcase, and we need to talk to the nurse before we take you home in that nice van your daddy bought." She spoke as if Scott were a baby.

"Tell Skye to quit *looking*!" Scott said, struggling to spit out his angry words.

"I'm not," Skye protested, her heart pounding. "And anyway, what am I supposed to do, keep my eyes shut for the rest of my life?"

"Yes!" Scott shouted.

"Why don't you go wait outside in the hall, Skye," her

father told her hurriedly. "Just humor me," he added in a whisper. "I guess Scott feels self-conscious about the way he looks, or something."

"Well, that's not *my* fault," Skye whispered back, but she felt relieved as she slid from Scott's emotion-jangled room into the brightly lit hallway. She slumped gratefully into a green vinyl chair and closed her eyes.

Three whole days with Scott. What were they letting themselves in for?

"Skye," a pleased-sounding voice said. "Just the girl I wanted to see."

Skye reluctantly opened her eyes. In front of her stood Scott's social worker, Ms. Santina who seemed nice enough.

"I wanted a word with you before Scott goes home," Ms. Santina said, and Skye found herself following the woman down the hall and into her determinedly cheerful office.

Ms. Santina

"Sit down, Skye," Ms. Santina said, smiling. "So, how are things going?"

"Great," Skye said cautiously.

"Scott's going home for a couple of days, and you probably have some questions about that," Ms. Santina said, looking sympathetic and attentive in advance.

"Not really," Skye said, shrugging. "I mean, I'm glad and everything," she added, lying.

Ms. Santina waited, but Skye didn't say anything more. "Have your parents explained to you exactly what happened to Scott, and what to expect from here on out?" the woman finally asked.

"Not really," Skye said again. "They've been a little busy," she added, in case she'd sounded critical.

To Skye's surprise, Ms. Santina threw back her head and laughed. "Understatement of the year," she finally said. "To put it simply, Skye, Scott suffered what is considered a moderate brain injury. When he crashed the car, the impact caused his brain to slam forward into his skull, and then sort of bounce back and forth, like a yolk getting knocked around inside a raw egg. So there was internal swelling of the brain at both sites of impact, and some internal bleeding. The pressure built up inside his brain while he was unconscious—which was probably for about half an hour or so, it's hard to tell exactly. Surgery was necessary to reduce that pressure, of course, and stop any further damage from happening."

"But he's not okay yet," Skye said, stating the obvious.

"Well, no, he's not," Ms. Santina said. "He's progressing nicely, but there's still some memory loss, which is very common with brain injuries, and some cognitive problems, in addition to the physical injuries Scott suffered in the accident."

"What kind of problems?" Skye asked, frowning.

"There's some language impairment," Ms. Santina said. "Reading and writing are difficult for your brother at this point, but we expect that to improve in time. But he also has problems with verbal communication, and that makes him feel very frustrated. He'll use inappropriate words, and so on."

"You mean swearing?" Skye asked. "Because he did that before. A *lot*."

"Not that kind of inappropriate," Ms. Santina said, smiling again. "I mean more like mixing his words up in a pretty significant way. So, let's see," she continued, glancing down at some notes. "Scott will have to have more speech therapy, once he comes home for good. And occupational therapy, and physical therapy, too. He'll need a lot of help."

"My mom can't do all that," Skye said, her voice shaking a little. "She hates making dinner, even. I think maybe Scott should just stay here with you guys."

"He can't," Ms. Santina said. "I totally hear you, Skye. It's just that the lucky ones get to a point where they can go home and continue their rehab there. There will be thera-

Me, Skye.

I am trying to take this in.

pists coming over to help out, though. Don't you worry about that."

"You think Scott is one of the lucky ones?" Skye asked, struggling to make it sound like a casual question.

"I do," Ms. Santina said, nodding. "But I want to prepare you for what to expect over the next few months. Scott is aware he's been in an accident, but only because we've told him so. He doesn't remember much about it, though, and he doesn't really know yet how serious it was."

"Huh," Skye said, trying to take it all in. "But this not-remembering stuff is just for now, right? It's not forever. He's gonna get all better, right?"

"Well, not *all* better," Ms. Santina said cautiously. "It remains to be seen how far his recovery will take him."

"But—but we've done everything the doctors said," Skye argued.

"Even so," Ms. Santina said, her voice gentle.

"So does that mean Scott's, like, *retarded* now?" Skye made herself ask the question. "No matter how hard he works at getting better?"

"Not at all," Ms. Santina said. "But Scott has a lot of

challenges to face. He'll probably be frustrated at times—with other people *and* himself. And he'll be depressed."

"Like I said, that's kind of the way he was before," Skye said.

"Well, multiply that by ten," Ms. Santina told her. "It's going to be tough, Skye."

"I really think he'd be better off staying here," Skye repeated, louder this time.

"Let's see how he does during the trial visit home," Ms. Santina said, glancing at her watch and getting to her feet—which obviously meant their time together was over, Skye realized, kissing about a thousand questions good-bye. "Good luck, Skye," Ms. Santina said, reaching out to take her hand. "And remember to take care of *yourself*."

"Sure, okay," Skye said, shaking hands. "And thanks for helping my brother. I'm sorry if he was ever rude to you or anything. He didn't mean it."

"You don't have to make excuses for him, Skye," Ms. Santina said, frowning a little. "I know you two are pretty close, but Scott's on his path now, and you're on yours. And both paths are equally important."

"Did he say we were close?" Skye asked, genuinely curious—because they hadn't been, not for years.

"He said you guys were like this," Ms. Santina said, smiling, and she held two fingers together.

"Huh," Skye said, trying to mask her expression—because she and Scott weren't *"like this"* at all before the accident.

They were *like that.*

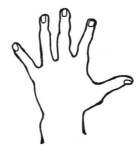

3

To Say Good-bye

"**S**o how come you're the one who has to move in with your grandmother in California, when it's Scott who has all the problems?" Skye's friend Hana asked a month later as they walked through the air-conditioned mall. The Albuquerque school year was going to start in less than a week, and Hana was supposed to be hunting for bargains. "I thought he was getting better," she added, frowning.

"He *is* getting better, I guess," Skye said, sighing. "He has his ups and downs, though, and lately there have been more downs than ups."

That was putting it mildly, she thought, remembering her brother's most recent scenes: yelling at the visiting physical therapist, a muscle-bound blond guy in his late twenties who remained stubbornly cheerful even as Scott's curses echoed throughout the house; refusing to read aloud to Skye as part of his speech therapy, or to practice his keyboarding; nagging their mom for junk food snacks, even though he wasn't getting any exercise and was definitely putting on weight.

His friends had mostly stopped coming by to see him — that was one problem, Skye thought. Well, it was summer, she told herself, and everyone was busy, and Scott's accident was old news by now. He was no longer everyone's pet accident victim; kids had moved on to other things.

BEFORE SCOTT'S ACCIDENT

1. Not only did he stop being fun when he was 12, he started being awful.
2. I didn't even like to invite friends over, because ANYTHING COULD HAPPEN.
3. I got headaches from GRITTING MY TEETH so hard!
4. And Mom + Dad started fighting a lot.
5. Of course, that could be a COINCIDENCE.
6. But it probably isn't.

But worst of all, Stacie had broken up with Scott — even though they weren't officially boyfriend and girlfriend.

But she'd wanted to make sure he, and everyone, knew it was over before school started. Skye couldn't really blame Stacie for that, even though Stacie had chosen e-mail as the way to let Scott know.

That was pretty brutal.

And then there were Scott's nightmares—though they sometimes came in the middle of the day. Like last week, for example. *"Eee-yahhhh,"* he'd suddenly roared, waking from a nap in front of the TV and throwing his head back as he howled.

Skye had raced into the family room, her heart thudding.

"No, no, *no*," Scott shouted. *"Nonononono-o-o!"* He hid his face, as if trying to protect it—from an invisible car's tumble through the desert night, Skye guessed.

"You're okay, Scotty," she yelled, stepping back a little because she was so frightened. "This isn't really happening."

Only—the accident *was* happening again, obviously. For him, anyway.

Where was her mom? Crying in the laundry room, like that other time?

No, she'd gone to the store, Skye remembered suddenly.

And her father was supposed to have come home early from work today, but there was no sign of him.

(Boy, *that* had caused a fight when Skye's mom got home! And by the time the fight was over, it had been decided that Skye should move to Sierra Madre, California, for the semester.)

Skye had tried to grab Scott's sleeve, and to her horror, he actually took a swing at her. Her own big brother! And suddenly Skye was absolutely furious—at Scott, for trying to hit her, even though he didn't really know he was doing it, and at her mom and dad, for leaving her alone with her crazy brother, and—

My meltdown...

...during Scott's meltdown.

"Look out!" Scott had cried, and he crumpled onto the sofa once more, panting. He covered his eyes with both hands and tried to curl up into a ball.

Skye counted to three, afraid to go near him.

Then Scott looked up and saw her for the first time. His now-pudgy face was streaked with tears, and he looked confused. "When is Mom coming home?" he asked.

"Pretty soon, Scotty. Pretty soon," some stranger inside

her had managed to reply—in the calmest voice anyone ever heard.

"Look at that skirt," Hana was saying now, nudging Skye in the ribs. "Wake up! What do you think?"

"It's cute," Skye said, trying unsuccessfully to picture the patchwork denim mini on Hana, who was both taller and rounder than Skye.

"I'm gonna try it on," Hana said, excited.

"Wow," Skye said. "Would your mom let you wear something that short, Hana?" she asked. "Even if the principal will?"

World's Smallest Patchwork Skirt

(no offense or anything, but NO WAY is Hana gonna be able to walk in this.)

"She'll get used to it," Hana said, grabbing Skye by the hand and dragging her into the store, which was practically shaking with music.

A few minutes later, the two girls were crammed into a dressing room, the flimsy curtain barely shielding them as Hana wrestled herself into the too-tight skirt. "Want me

⟩*SPECIAL STUFF ABOUT*⟨ HANA and ME

1. We wear (almost) the same size!
2. We both love purple and orange!
3. We both hate SCARY movies!

4. But we love chocolate ice cream!
5. And stuffed animals!

to get you another size?" Skye asked, carefully not saying *"bigger,"* because Hana liked being the same size as her. It was one of their things.

"No, this is perfect," Hana replied, attempting to tug the hem down a little. "Don't you think? I am definitely getting this," she said, narrowing her eyes and looking both determined and ready to fight. "You should tell your mom and dad you don't want to go," she added, as if she were completing the last part of the same thought.

"They already bought my plane ticket," Skye said softly, still looking in the mirror at her friend. "I leave in two more days. They want me to get all settled in with Gran in Sierra Madre before school starts. But it's only temporary, Hana. I'll be back soon."

"How soon?" Hana asked, frowning.

"Thanksgiving vacation, for sure," Skye said. "And Christmas, too. I'll be home for good by the time next semester starts. That's the plan, anyway."

Hana steadied herself against Skye as she wriggled out of the skirt. "Too bad my mom's so strict about me using my cell, ever since that famous bill, or I'd call you at *least* every morning and every night," she said, panting a little.

"We can always text," Skye told her.

"Nope," Hana said, shaking her head. "They've started charging, like, fifteen cents apiece for receiving or sending a text message, and my mom says that could add up to, like, a couple of dollars a day, easy, just for you and me. So that's out, too."

"Well, what about e-mail?" Skye asked.

"We could do that, I guess," Hana said, sounding a little gloomy, because she hated what she called "*normal writing*," as opposed to texting.

"You have to promise, Hana," Skye said, turning to face her. "I'm going to be stuck all alone in California while my real life is happening here, without me."

"Okay," Hana said, relenting. "I promise I'll write."

"It sucks to say good-bye," Skye said softly.

"It totally does," Hana agreed.

But her friend's attention had already wandered, Skye saw with dismay, and Hana was caressing her new skirt, obviously imagining her first day at Taft—a day when Skye would be attempting to build some sort of life in an unreal alternate universe, in a completely different world.

"Thanks for nothing, Scott," Skye whispered.

☆❀ AFTER SCOTT'S ACCIDENT ❀☜

1. Our lives have been turned UPSIDE DOWN.
   (That is not just an expression.)
2. I even have to move!
3. All my family's extra money and energy goes to Scott.
4. There is nothing left for me, not that I am complaining.
5. But would he do the same for ONE OF US?
6. Hah! I don't THINK so.
7. What will he be like if he gets better?
8. And what about if he DOESN'T ??

SIERRA MADRE

4

Eucalyptus Terrace

Skye stifled a yawn as she sneaked a sideways look at her grandmother. In spite of living in Southern California her whole life, Gran hated freeway driving and didn't mind saying so. "Stay awake, darling," Gran said, not taking her eyes off the road.

"Okay," Skye said, trying to look alert.

Wow, she thought, pretending to keep an eye on the traffic whizzing past them on the left. This whole California thing was going to be weird—because having a nice, jolly grandmother come to visit in Albuquerque for a few days over Thanksgiving,

GRAN

the world's largest nutritional expert!

or meeting up with her at the Grand Canyon for a family vacation, was different from moving in with her all alone for an entire semester.

Gran was Skye's father's mother. She had faded brown hair that sprang from her head in determined curls, and blue eyes, and a big grandmotherly lap, in spite of her interest in both exercise and healthy eating. In fact, Skye thought, Gran might be the world's largest nutritional expert—which sounded like a put-down, but it wasn't. Skye thought pulling something like that off was awesome.

It was like being a teenage girl—Scott's ex-girlfriend Stacie, say—who wasn't really pretty but hypnotized everyone into thinking that she was. Or being the guy who wore ugly clothes that everyone thought were cool. Or being the kid at school who came up with a quirky trademark so off-the-wall that in normal life, people would think maybe they should cross the street to get away from him, but everyone just totally accepted it.

Skye, on the other hand, had formulated a plan during the two-hour flight from Albuquerque, New Mexico, to Los Angeles, California: she would not draw attention to herself in any way, shape, or form during her stay. Her goal for this semester was either to blend in perfectly, or, better, to become invisible.

"Almost home," her grandmother said. The houses seemed to crawl by in a slow-motion blur as the Toyota climbed the hill toward Sierra Madre, and Eucalyptus Terrace. "Can you spell 'eucalyptus'?" Gran asked, relaxing her grip on the wheel just a little as she signaled to make a left-hand turn.

Skye smiled. "I live in Albuquerque, Gran," she told her grandmother. "I can spell anything."

"Oh, right," Gran said, smiling. "Just making conversation, really. But you're so quiet, darling. Are you thinking about poor Scott?"

"No," Skye said, turning her head and looking out of the window once more. There were enough people thinking about *"poor Scott"* to last a lifetime, weren't there? "We're here," she said as her grandmother turned into what looked like a wide driveway, but was really a very short dead-end street.

"Finally," Gran said, her Toyota creeping to the end of the street. "Wave hello to Maddy, Skye. She lives across the street now, and she'll be in your grade at school."

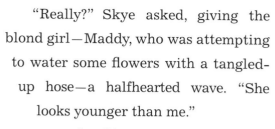

Oh boy. Oh boy. I have a neighbor.

"Really?" Skye asked, giving the blond girl—Maddy, who was attempting to water some flowers with a tangled-up hose—a halfhearted wave. "She looks younger than me."

"We'll talk about that some other time," Gran said, pulling into her driveway. She clambered stiffly out of the car and stretched. "Now, let's get you settled in, darling. You can check your e-mail after you unpack."

⊚

HI SKYE. U R MY K-BRDING 2 DAY + THEN I HAVE PT. MOM IS SLPNG + DAD IS AT WRK. THIS SUX SCOTT

"What does he have to say?" Gran asked, bustling into her tiny home office.

"He says hi," Skye reported. "And that I'm his keyboarding assignment today. Then he has physical therapy. And my mom is sleeping, and my dad is still at work."

"Well, that's good, isn't it?" Gran said, peering over her shoulder—which was something that was not going to fly once Hana started writing, Skye thought, trying to hide her irritation. "You can almost understand what he's trying to say," Gran added.

"It's a lot better than the way he was typing last month, anyway," Skye told her.

"He'll improve in leaps and bounds, you'll see," Gran said, patting Skye on the back. "Don't worry, Skye. He'll get better every single day."

Skye frowned, not knowing how to reply—because that wasn't what the social worker told her a couple of weeks earlier, talking about Scott. She'd said, "It'll be two steps forward, one step back. That's on a good day, Skye. And there's no knowing yet how far he'll be able to go."

But there was no point in telling Gran that, Skye decided, signing off. At least one person in the family should be allowed to remain an optimist.

5

Very, Very, Very, Very Nervous

HI SKYE. I WALKD LAPS IN THE POOL AT LOONIES. SCHOOL
STARTED NOONE COMES TO SEE ME EVEN JERMY. BUT JT
WRKS HERE NOW HES COOL. U R MY KEBORDING 2 DAY.
MOM HRT HER BACK IT SUX. FROM SCOTT

⑥

HI SKYE. I HAD A SEZURE, THAT SUX. DAD SAY MOM
FREKD OUT BUT I DONT REMBER IT. FROM SCOTT

⑥

Hi, Scott. Congratulations about walking laps in the pool.
Gran says hi. From Skye

⑥

Hey, Hana! How's it going at Taft? Did you get to wear your

new skirt? I'm bored times three, bored bored bored. School starts next week and I am very, very, very, very nervous. Scott is doing great and I am sure I will get to come home soon.

Luv, Skye

Hi Skye! School is going ok. Soooooo busy here but miss U lots. Luv U, Hana

6

First Day of School

"You should eat a more substantial breakfast, darling," Gran told Skye the first day of school, representatives from all the known food groups arrayed around her own breakfast plate like an admiring audience. "A multigrain toaster waffle, at least," she suggested, peering at Skye's half-eaten energy bar with suspicion. "Maybe with a little apple butter on it."

"I'm too nervous to eat that much," Skye said, sliding her sketchbook into her book bag, having pasted an ordinary spiral notebook cover onto the front the night before to make it less noticeable. A secret artist was the best kind to be, Skye had decided—especially if

Skye McPhee

the invisible girl

you wanted to be invisible in a brand-new school. That way, you could draw exactly what you wanted to draw, the way you wanted to draw it.

Art was something no one could take away from you, no matter *where* the grown-ups in your life made you move.

Gran leaned back in her chair and gave Skye a smile so wide that her face creased like the top of a dinner roll. "You're excited, not nervous," she informed Skye. "But it's the same thing, scientifically speaking."

"I'm pretty sure I'm nervous, Gran," Skye objected, secretly annoyed.

Gran shrugged. "If you want to argue with science," she said, carefully layering cheese and turkey on a piece of toast.

"I'd better go," Skye told her, looking away before she hurled—because, scientifically speaking, that's what she thought she was about to do.

"But it's just a fifteen-minute walk to school," Gran protested, the sagging piece of toast halfway to her mouth. "And Maddy isn't here yet. I thought you two could walk to school together," she added, looking pleased with herself. "You've both been through orientation, but it'll be nice to have some company the first day, won't it?"

"*Maddy?*" Skye asked, startled. True, they'd been hanging out a little over the past three weeks, the way you're basically forced to do with neighbor kids your same age, but Skye had already seen Maddy freak out twice so far: once when a favorite TV show was canceled for a news conference, and once when Maddy's dad mistakenly brought home pizza with green peppers on it, which Maddy said ruined the entire pizza for good.

"I just like things to be right," Maddy had tried to explain when that pizza crisis was over.

"Well, everyone does," Skye replied, struggling to keep her voice steady.

"Yes, but I *need* things to be right," Maddy had insisted.

What was up with Maddy? Skye didn't know, and all Gran would tell her was, "*Everyone's got something they have to deal with, and so does Maddy.*"

Maybe so, Skye thought now—but she knew she wanted to be alone when she first walked into her temporary new school. Because how was she supposed to blend in, or better yet, be invisible, with someone as unpredictable as Maddy attached to her side?

It was just too risky.

"Look, Gran, we *can't* walk to school together," Skye exclaimed. "You should have asked me first," she added, so angry that she felt as if she was about to start crying. "I wanted to walk to school alone today. And I can choose my own friends, by the way, if I even want to bother having any in Sierra Madre, which I don't! Just because Maddy and I are the same age, that doesn't mean—"

Gran had put down her toast and was gazing at Skye, seemingly stunned, when the doorbell rang. "That'll be Maddy," Gran said softly.

"Oh, all right. Have it your way," Skye yelled, and she grabbed her book bag and slammed out of the warm, cozy kitchen, leaving her grandmother staring after her in confusion and dismay.

"Okay, we're here," Skye said after what felt like the longest, most silent fifteen minutes of her life. "You have your schedule, right? And you know where your locker is?"

"Yes," Maddy said. A warm breeze ruffled her medium-short hair, which was pretty and blond, but Maddy had worn a T-shirt with a babyish cartoon character on the front—in spite of the obvious fact that she clearly wasn't a baby.

"Well, okay then," Skye said as kids of every size, shape, and description shoved past them, stampeding herdlike up the school's front steps. "See you."

"At two forty-five P.M.," Maddy said in her usual precise way.

Skye bit her lip and wished her grandmother had heard this. *See what you've done?* she felt like saying to Gran. "But if I don't show up, Maddy," Skye said, trying to be nice, "just walk home alone, okay? Don't wait around for me."

"No, I'll be right here, Skye," Maddy said, staring at the ground. "I don't mind waiting for extended periods of time."

Skye sighed, then turned away and stomped up the steps, heading for her locker. Her assigned locker was on the first floor, in the main hallway, and she'd practiced unlocking it several times after orientation, having easily memorized the combination.

Today, however, she couldn't get it to open.

"I think that one's mine," a squeaky voice said in her ear. "Number fifty-seven." It was a confident-looking girl Skye had noticed at orientation.

squeaky girl

51

Just what I needed today...

"Oh," Skye said, blushing. "I'm sorry. I thought it said fifty-one."

"No big deal," the girl said, shrugging. "We can trade, if this is your lucky number or something."

"I didn't *want* this one," Skye tried to explain. "I just made a mistake, that's all. See how the numbers are sort of funny?"

"Well, no big deal," the girl said again, after peering politely at the numbers, and Skye crept off to her locker feeling like the biggest fool in the world.

She spent so long pretending to be busy at her locker, trying to regain her composure, that the hall was nearly empty when she finally looked up. Suddenly, a noisy group of boys tumbled down the stairs like a mini avalanche, and they began pushing and shoving their way through the hall, seeming to pick up speed as they went. The boys—five or six of them—churned past Skye without even seeing her, but Maddy was standing frozen in their path just a few yards away.

Maddy had been watching her, Skye realized, startled, but she hadn't known enough to get out of the boys' way.

"Hey, it's a girl," one of the boys said, stumbling against Maddy and grabbing hold of her arm—to steady himself, Skye thought, but she couldn't be sure. The boys were

UH-OH.

crowding around Maddy now, and it was difficult to see what was happening.

"He finally got a girl," a second boy said, laughing. "Even if it is just a sixth-grader."

"Go ahead, Cord," the biggest boy said. "Let's hear you talk some game!"

"Give it up," a fourth boy said in a drawling, too-cool voice. "She's a *re*-tard."

"Ease up, Aaron," a different boy protested.

Skye wanted to do something to shut them up, or at least to make the first boy let go of Maddy, but she couldn't move. Everything was happening so fast that it didn't seem real. Maybe she truly *was* invisible, Skye thought suddenly. After all, those boys hadn't seen her, and—

But no. Maddy saw her. The girl's brown eyes were dark

with fear, and Skye took a concrete-footed step forward in spite of herself.

And, as if they were one, the boys turned to look at Skye just as the warning bell rang. "Aw, let her loose," the biggest boy said, pulling the first boy—Aaron?—away from Maddy. "Let's go, dude, or they're gonna sweat us."

And like that, the avalanche of boys melted away.

Skye and Maddy looked at each other for one long, white-faced moment, and then Skye turned away—ashamed, and angry with Maddy, though she couldn't have said why.

7

Social Ecology

S kye hid in the girls' room for almost twenty minutes
after school let out, hoping Maddy would walk home
alone, but Maddy was still waiting for her at the bottom of
the school's front steps a little after three. "Hello, Skye,"
she said, not seeming irritated at all by the delay. And,
in spite of what had happened in the hall that morning,
Maddy looked cheerful.

"Hi," Skye mumbled, trying to look around without
moving her head, to see who else was on the steps. "You
could've left without me, you know."

"I would never do that," Maddy said softly.

Skye sighed as they began their walk home. She did
not want to spend the entire semester walking to and from
school with Maddy, but she felt too drained by her first day

at Amelia Earhart to pursue the topic. Also, she admitted privately, she felt guilty about what had happened in the hallway that morning. Should she have said something to those boys? Tried to protect Maddy somehow?

"Are you angry with me for some reason, Skye?" Maddy asked after a few blocks, sounding more curious than worried.

"Why would I be angry?" Skye asked, not answering Maddy's question.

"I don't know the answer to that," Maddy said, plodding along.

Skye counted to ten. "Who were those boys?" she finally asked Maddy. "The ones who grabbed you this morning?"

"They bumped into me," Maddy corrected her. "It was a collision. An accident. Only one of them is really mean, Skye. He's in the eighth grade. He grabbed my arm last summer when I was just walking down the road, and he bumped into my—my front. That was probably only an accident, too. But he calls me names pretty often. He almost made me cry once."

"Which one?" Skye asked.

"'Re-tard,'" Maddy said, pro-

MADDY EXPLAINING
STUFF.

nouncing the word carefully as she answered the wrong question. "Only I'm not, actually. I'm something else. So he's mistaken."

"What do you mean, you're something else?" Skye asked in what she hoped was a casual tone of voice. "Are you saying you have, like, a learning disability?"

"No," Maddy said, shaking her curly head. "Learning's easy for me. I get really good grades. It's the people who are hard! Except for you," she added quickly, as if not wanting to hurt Skye's feelings. "You're different, Skye."

"Well, thanks, I *guess*," Skye said. "But I don't get it, Maddy. What do you mean, the people are hard?"

Maddy frowned, obviously planning her reply. "Other kids sometimes think I'm strange, right?" she finally said, not really asking. "Like those boys this morning. And hardly anyone talks to me at school, but my counselor is helping me with that. She says I should just say hi to people first, and ask them how they're doing," she added.

"But what does your counselor say is the matter with you?" Skye asked, hoping the question wasn't too rude.

"Nothing's the matter with me, but I have a *syndrome*," Maddy said, sounding both important and a little mysterious. "That means like a pattern of symptoms—but not symptoms like being sick," she assured Skye.

"That's good," Skye said weakly. "But I think you

should tell people, Maddy. Because maybe then they'd leave you alone," she said, thinking of those boys in the hall.

"Do you tell people everything that's different about you?" Maddy asked, sounding curious once more.

"Well, no," Skye admitted, thinking of her sketch-book—and, of course, her brother. And the fights her mom and dad were having. "I guess I don't."

"Me either," Maddy said, smiling. "So we're very similar, Skye!"

"Sort of, anyway," Skye admitted. "But—but who was that boy who grabbed you this morning?"

"That was Cord Driscoll," Maddy said quietly. "He and Aaron Petterson are friends. Aaron is the mean one, Danko Marshall is the big, scary-looking one, and Kee Williams is the other one."

"You should have gotten out of the way," she told Maddy. "This morning, I mean."

"I couldn't," Maddy said. "I was worried about you, Skye."

"Worried?" Skye asked, shocked. "About *me*? Why?"

"Because you were just standing there and standing there, with your head inside your empty locker," Maddy said. "I thought maybe you were stuck."

"I wasn't stuck," Skye replied softly, hiding an embarrassed smile. "Look, Maddy," she said. "You have to get out of the way when boys go running through the hall like that. Especially eighth-grade boys."

"They weren't *all* in the eighth grade," Maddy argued. "The boy who told Aaron to ease up this morning is Kee Williams, who is sometimes pretty nice. He's just in the seventh grade, but he's on the same football team as the older boys, so he hangs out with them. It's an honor for him, I guess."

"How do you know all this stuff about everyone?" Skye asked, truly curious.

Maddy shrugged. "Sierra Madre's a small town," she told Skye. "Everyone pretty much knows everyone else, except for the new people."

"Well, I might be new," Skye said, "but I'm right about getting out of the way when boys run by, Maddy."

"Why? Because they're bigger than us, and they might knock us over?"

Dear Maddy,

"Well, yeah," Skye said. "And also because they're *boys*."

"But that's not fair," Maddy said, frowning as they turned into Eucalyptus Terrace. "I'm a member of the planet Earth just like them. I'm just as much a human being as they are."

The planet Earth doesn't even know we are members. Sincerely yours, Skye

"Not in middle school you aren't," Skye mumbled, but she wouldn't repeat herself when Maddy asked what she'd just said.

⊚

Hi, Mom! Thanks for calling! Here is some stuff I forgot to say. I got my fine arts elective after all! It is fourth period. There are some art kids who are nice, and Gran seems relieved that I fit in at least somewhere in what she calls the social ecology of our school.

I hope your back is better. Say hi to Dad for me, okay? And Scott, too.

Love, Skye

P.S. Is Hana okay? I have only heard from her once, but don't say anything if you see her. She's probably just busy with other stuff.

⊚

Hey, Hana! School started today, but it was boring, and the kids here are boring, too. I wish I was home instead of doing time in Sierra Madre, but you can't have everything, I guess. Write and cheer me up, okay? Luv, Skye (your friend, remember?)

some
Art Class Kids

Amanda

Jamila

Pip

Matteo

8

The Thing about Art

In spite of what she'd written to Hana two weeks earlier, the days seemed to be flying by. It was now Monday morning, the last week in September, and Skye was sitting on Amelia Earhart's wide front steps pretending to study as she secretly drew the kids around her, an act that was almost making them seem real.

The kids at Amelia Earhart were okay, Skye thought as she sketched, if you didn't count those football players in the hall—or their admirers, the bad ballerinas, who had earned their name in part,

the Bad Ballerinas
have a conversation!

Skye had learned, by tying the ribbons of old toe shoes together and tossing the pale pink satin shoes over telephone wires up by the canyon, to claim that neighborhood as their own.

But every school probably had girls like that—even Taft Middle School in Albuquerque, New Mexico.

She'd ask Hana, if she ever got the chance.

Hana had only e-mailed that one time, though, and she hadn't said much. Miffed, Skye had decided to cut back on her own e-mails to Hana—a decision that ended up being a lose-lose situation, Skye admitted privately. But she'd be back to her real life in Albuquerque soon, and then she could smooth things out.

Skye sighed, and she was looking at one of her drawings as Kee Williams, the maybe-nice seventh-grader, walked by. He was tall, thin, and cute, with dark brown hair, and eyes the color of her grandmother's morning tea.

Had he looked her way? Probably not, Skye decided, surprised to find herself feeling a little disappointed. But things weren't all bad, because after lunch she'd be going to her favorite class of all at Amelia Earhart Middle School: art.

The thing about art wasn't so much the actual art you made, in Skye's opinion. It was more that when you were making that art, time stood still and you forgot about everything: about the fun Hana might be having without you back in Albuquerque; about how weird it still felt to be living with Gran in Sierra Madre; even about your messed-up family, especially Scott, whose rehab seemed to have stalled.

She was still Scott's keyboarding assignment, as he kept reminding her.

"Hey, Skye," a helium voice belonging to Amanda Berrigan—the first school day's locker mix-up girl—said. "What's that?" Amanda tried to get a look at the carefully disguised sketchbook disappearing into Skye's book bag.

"English," Skye said, deliberately vague, even though Amanda was in her art class, and Skye was starting to like her. "I was just finishing up an assignment."

Amanda Berrigan was a little taller than Skye, and slightly plump, with red-blond hair that seemed to glow with its own light. In spite of her bouncy walk and squeaky voice, however, Amanda proudly claimed to have what she called a "dark inner life."

But Amanda was pretty cool. She was even nice to

Maddy, who by now was something of a before-and-after-school fixture in Skye's life, and who the art kids, at least, were gradually coming to accept.

"Skye-ster," another voice said. It was Pip Claymore, another art kid Skye had been privately calling *Pipe Cleaner* in her sketchbook, because he was so skinny.

"Got your maps all ready for Ms. O'Hare?" Amanda asked Pip and Skye. Ms. O'Hare's assignment had been to draw a detailed map—of anything at all. "I did a map of my dream life," Amanda said in a hushed voice, not waiting for their answers. She tweaked her bright hair, and, as she closed her blue eyes, sparkly slashes of turquoise eye shadow caught the sunlight. "My dream life is very grim, so prepare yourselves," she whispered.

"Well, of course it's grim," Pip said, the corner of his mouth twisted up in an ironic smile. "Your *life* is grim, what with all the riding lessons and cell phones and makeup and fancy clothes and everything."

"What did you do for the project, Pip?" Skye asked him, before Amanda could explode.

"I drew a map of my face," Pip said, grimacing. "Including my freckles and zits. It's kind of a connect-the-dots thing. What about you?"

"I drew a map of Sierra Madre," Skye said, suddenly thinking maybe that hadn't been such a great idea.

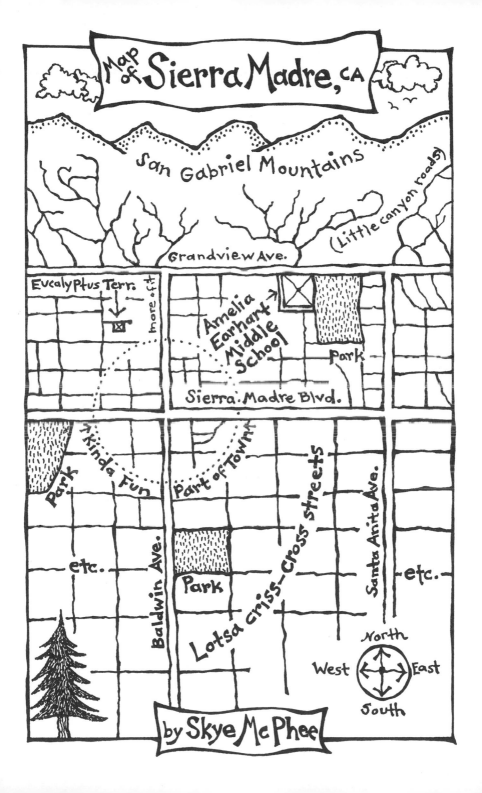

8th grade "lima-bean eyes" Aaron picks on 6th grade "pipe cleaner" Pip.

YEAH, that's a fair fight !!!

Kids surged around them, because first period was about to start. "Move it, art jerks," Aaron Petterson called out as he shoved past them. He jabbed his black notebook into Pip's ribs, and his lima-bean eyes gleamed with malice.

"Jock itch," Pip mumbled to the boy's back.

And just as if a reverse switch had been thrown, Aaron backed up. "What did you say to me?" he roared over the din of the kids around them. And then he used a word that made everyone turn and look.

Skye was shocked by Aaron's use of that ugly word, grounds for a quick march to the principal's office back home in Albuquerque, at the very least. Still, kids seemed to say it all the time—without even thinking about it, like it was a kind of all-purpose insult. Which made the word meaningless and boring, in a weird way.

"What did you say?" Aaron asked again, challenging Pip.

"Nothing," Pip mumbled, looking away.

"You better believe it, *nothing*," Aaron said loudly, looking around for an audience. "Pipsqueak. Pansy." No one but Pip, Amanda, and Skye was listening to him, though, so he stopped reciting his list of insults. "You better watch it," he warned Pip, and then he was gone.

"I miss him already," Amanda said sarcastically.

"See you in art, jerks," Pip said to Amanda and Skye, laughing a little shakily as he echoed Aaron's intended insult.

"Yeah. See you, art jerks," Skye said, smiling, and the sting somehow drained away from what Aaron had said as they claimed those words as their own.

9

Temporary

"**E**xcellent, people," Ms. O'Hare said a few hours later as her art class surveyed the maps tacked up on the room's wide bulletin board. She fluffed her wavy bangs and smoothed the long ponytail that curled over one shoulder and surveyed her students' first independent project. "Just excellent." She smiled, and her eyes shone.

Jamila Westmoreland raised her hand and waggled her long brown fingers to attract Ms. O'Hare's attention. "Are we going to vote on them, to see which one is the best?" she asked when Ms. O'Hare called on her.

Ms. O'Hare looked momentarily

confused. "Vote on them?" she asked. "This is not a contest, Jamila. This is art."

Jamila—and a few other kids—looked disappointed.

"But I do have an announcement to make," Ms. O'Hare said, as if that might cheer up her more competitive students. "I've been asked to start an after-school art activities group, to take care of all the art chores the school evidently thought we'd be doing in this class."

It was Ms. O'Hare's first year here, too, Skye had learned.

Matteo Molina's arm shot up. "What kind of art chores?" he asked when Ms. O'Hare called his name. He sounded a little suspicious. "Like cleaning out brushes and stuff?"

"No," Ms. O'Hare said, shaking her head. "More like making posters and banners, and working on the special newspaper for Homecoming, complete with the famous insert of the football players, and so on. It'll be mostly lettering, some cut-and-paste, and a little computer work, of course, but there should be some creativity involved. It'll be fun," she promised—sounding unconvinced herself.

But it did sound like fun, at least to Skye. It would be something to do after school, anyway.

"So, how many of you can I count on for, say, at least once a week? Or twice weekly, when we get closer to Homecoming?" Ms. O'Hare asked, clearly not expecting anyone to volunteer.

"Do we get extra credit?" a voice asked from the rear of the class.

"No," Ms. O'Hare said, shaking her head. "Just my undying gratitude. And it might help preserve the *real* art class someday, if I can prove we're actually useful to the school."

"Well, I can't do it, except for Tuesdays and Thursdays," Jamila announced to the class. "Because of track."

"And I have gymnastics Mondays, Wednesdays, and Fridays," Matteo said.

"How about Tuesdays?" Ms. O'Hare said, an expression of hope mingled with surprise on her face. "And then maybe we can add Thursdays later on, if it becomes necessary. I should be able to get you all out of here by four thirty or so. May I see a show of hands, please?"

Skye slowly raised her hand, worrying a little about Maddy as she did so. It could prove to be a long walk home for her neighbor, if she had to go alone.

Amanda's hand went up, too, as did Pip's, Jamila's, and Matteo's.

"That's five," Ms. O'Hare said, sounding pleased. "Why, that's excellent, people. Any questions?" she asked.

Kids sneaked glances at the clock—the bell was about to ring—and shook their heads.

"All right, then," Ms. O'Hare said, looking greatly relieved. "Please report for duty tomorrow afternoon at three, and we'll see what's on the agenda."

"Ms. O'Hare?" Skye asked after most of the art kids had bolted from class. "Can I ask you a question?"

"Of course, Skye," Ms. O'Hare said, looking up from stuffing her note-book into what looked like a gingham-lined feedbag. "What's up? Terrific map, by the way."

"Thanks," Skye said, blushing a little. "Um, I was

Kids always look at the clock before saying anything when the bell is about to ring!

just wondering if a girl who doesn't take art could be in art activities on Tuesday afternoons, too. Until I go back home to Albuquerque, that is," she added. "See, this girl—Maddy—lives on my grandmother's street, and we always walk home together."

"Until you go back home to Albuquerque?" Ms. O'Hare asked, instantly focusing on the wrong thing, in Skye's opinion. "But you're living here now, aren't you?"

"Not really," Skye said. "I mean, I'm here," she tried to explain, her eyes on the floor, "but I'm not really *here*, if you know what I mean. It's only temporary. Just until my big brother gets better."

"There's no such thing as 'only temporary,' Skye," Ms. O'Hare said quietly. "Unless you consider *everything* to be temporary, I suppose. Each moment in life is important, you know."

Oh, great, Skye thought. Just what she needed, a philosopher. "Excuse me, but I'm going to be late to my next class," she said, wishing she had never asked Ms. O'Hare about Maddy.

"Sorry," Ms. O'Hare said, scrabbling in the feedbag once more. "I'll write you a note. And of course your friend can join us after school. The more the merrier!"

Skye wanted to tell Ms. O'Hare that Maddy wasn't an official friend, not one that she'd chosen for herself, and that she wasn't especially artistic—or merry, for that matter. But she decided to keep her mouth shut.

"Thanks, Ms. O'Hare," was all she said.

10

Dear Scott

~~~~~~~

HI SKYE. U R MY KEBORDING 2-DAY. JT QUIT HE MOVED TO
WAKKO TXAS. MOM IS ALL SAD + DAD BUT ME THE MOST
B-CUS JT WAS MY ONLY FREND SINCE JERMY. IT USTO BE
DIFRENT NOW IT SUX. FROM SCOTT

◎

Dear Scott, I'm sorry JT had to quit, but Mom will hire
someone else to help out.

(By the way, I used to be your friend, a long time ago. And
things used to be different for me, too, in case you forgot!!!
And you don't have to keep saying I'm your keyboarding
assignment. I know that's the only reason you write me.) Skye

◎

Dear Scott, I'm sorry I was so mean in my e-mail yesterday. Some of the girls at Amelia Earhart are kind of snotty, especially Taylor Shusterman, who says I should try buying vintage, if I can't afford nice new clothes! You got me on a bad day. (Kids here think Sierra Madre is the center of the universe. Taylor even thinks New Mexico is not part of the USA and that Spanish is my native language. How dumb can you get?) From your sister, who is not a foreigner, Skye

⊚

HI SKYE, THATS OK. U R PRETTY WERD HAHA. TALOR IS A DUM NAME 4 A GIRL. IT IS COLD HERE, LAST YR I WAS PLANG FOTBALL. THIS YR I AM TRING TO WAK + NOT FALL OFER. FROM SCOTT

⊚

"How's Scott doing?" Gran asked Skye at dinner that night: turkey meat loaf with regular ketchup, for which Skye had had to negotiate in the supermarket aisle, steamed peas, spinach salad, and a whole-wheat roll. "Is his writing any better?"

"Well," Skye said, after pausing to take a sip of milk, "it was never all that great, even before the accident. But I guess he's improving,"

I hate it when grown-ups cry. It makes me feel shaky & scared...

she added. "At first, it took him so much time to type out a word that he usually forgot what it was."

Tears filled Gran's eyes, and Skye looked away, because grown-ups showing emotion was a thing she did not like to see.

"I'm so glad he has someone to write to, Skye," Gran said. "Someone who really cares about him."

"Writing to me is just part of his rehab," Skye objected quietly, poking through her salad with barely disguised suspicion—because she now knew that Gran liked to sneak extra nutrition into her dishes when least expected: tofu cubes, tempeh strips, nuts and seeds. She found these things tucked into her sandwiches and folded into omelets, as well as sprinkled onto her salads.

It was like being an unwilling member of some cult, Skye thought, longing suddenly for her mom's slapdash attempts at cooking: pre-cut cheese squares melted onto English muffins for dinner, or tortilla-wrapped hot dogs, or bright orange macaroni and cheese from a box.

And then there were last summer's salty, greasy take-out meals: sweet-and-sour *everything*, from that one Chinese restaurant that delivered; the family-sized buckets of spaghetti with meat sauce from their favorite Italian restaurant, complete with garlic bread, of course; and anything drive-through.

"And you really care about Maddy, too," Gran was saying thoughtfully. "That was so nice of you to include her in your art activities group, Skye. Maddy's mother says she's really blooming."

"You don't have to say that," Skye mumbled, because she didn't like talking about her friends behind their backs. Well, her *almost*-friend. "Maddy's doing great in art activities. Ms. O'Hare says she doesn't know what she'd do without her, because everyone else is such a diva."

> **☆❀ SOME THINGS ABOUT MADDY❀☆**
>
> 1. She is an only child.
> 2. She HATES loud noises.
> 3. But she loves watching the same DVDs and listening to the same CDs over and over.
> 4. She freaks out about food and funny smells.
> 5. Like tar, for instance.
> 6. This is because she is ⋛VERY SENSITIVE.⋚
> 7. But she is also a very loyal friend.
> 8. I also think she is BRAVE!
> 9. If I was scared of noise food and smells, I would probably just STAY HOME.

"Is there something the matter with your salad?" Gran asked suddenly.

"Uh, no," Skye replied. "Not really."

"'Not really' isn't exactly a ringing endorsement, Skye," Gran said.

"I'm sorry, Gran," Skye said, loading up her fork with spinach. "It's just that my mom makes salad differently, and I guess that's kind of what I'm used to."

Gran thought about this. "Well," she finally said, "what about if you plan the menu for tomorrow night? What sounds good? You name it."

Skye grinned at her. "How about beanie-weenies, and iceberg lettuce salad with orange bottled dressing?" she answered, thinking of home. "And a butterscotch pudding cup with whipped topping for dessert?"

A shocked silence seemed to hover over the dining-room table. "I hope you're joking," Gran finally said, barely squeezing out the words.

"Not really," Skye said softly. "But never mind. It's okay."

"I—I could try making the beanie-weenies, if you tell me how," Gran said, sounding brave. "And you can pour ketchup all over it," she added.

Skye managed a laugh. "Thanks, Gran," she said. "But the way you cook is okay. I'm getting used to it, in fact."

Dear Scott, Hi! Guess what? I think Gran has a boyfriend! She

had a date last night, and I had to go over to Maddy's house.

Maddy is this girl who lives across the street. She comes to art activities with me. She has a syndrome of some kind, but it doesn't seem to bother her much.

School is going okay. The meanest kids in school are on the football team. They pretty much leave us art kids alone, except when they feel like picking on someone, usually Pip. The bad ballerinas pick on Amanda and me, but so far it's not too bad. From Art Jerk Skye

HI ART JRK HAHA! THAT IS A MESSD UP NAME. AND NO WAY GRAN HAS A BFRND. SHE IS 2 OLD. I WNT 2 THE MALL WITH MOM AND I SAW STACIE BUT SHE PRETND SHE DOESNT SEE ME, THAT SUX RELLY BAD. I PRETND IM BUSY LOKING AT STUFF IN A STOR SO MOM WILL BE OK WITH IT.

It's Only Temporary

(DON'T GET MAD, U R MY KEYBRDNG TODAY BUT ID WRITE
U ANYWAY) LOVE SCOTT

Dear Scott, I am really sorry about Stacie at the mall. I think
you were a lot braver than Stacie, because you were thinking
about Mom, and Stacie wasn't thinking about anyone except
herself. Love, Skye

11

Sticky

As usual, Skye opened her locker with caution. It was two weeks before Halloween, and the tall narrow space was a mess, crammed full of textbooks, forgotten take-home announcements, stray assignments, a sweatshirt, and a couple of battered lip-gloss wands, among other things. But today, on top of her second-best hairbrush, was a folded piece of paper.

Skye hunched against her half-opened locker for privacy and unfolded the paper with fingers that had suddenly turned cold. Was this hate mail from one of the bad ballerinas, or just a note from Amanda?

But instead of being either, it was a really cool drawing—unsigned. It looked like a long, scary head with hollow eyes and a single listening ear, and it had ropy cords twining all

around it. The head's gaping mouth looked as if it was trying to say something.

It was a boy's drawing for sure, in Skye's opinion, but who had done it? Pip? Matteo? And why had whoever-it-was sneaked it into her locker?

Skye smoothed the drawing flat and slipped it into her school notebook.

"Urk! What are you eating?" Melissa Del Vecchio—one of the bad ballerinas—asked Amanda a couple of hours later, wrinkling her nose as she stalked by the art kids' cafeteria table. Skye looked down, her finger tracing cloudy circles on the beige laminated tabletop. She'd been thinking about the mystery drawing.

"It's called a peanut butter sandwich, Melissa," Amanda said in her squeaky voice, but with exaggerated patience. "Can you say 'sand-wich'?"

"No, I can't," Melissa replied, swinging her hair over her shoulder. "But I can say 'gross.' Do you know how many carbohydrates there are in that thing? And fat?"

"Nope, and neither

Fun at Lunch
(Part One)

do you," Amanda said, taking a defiant bite of her sticky sandwich—which effectively ended her part of the conversation.

"Well," Melissa said loudly, "it's not exactly like you *need* extra carbohydrates and fat, Amanda. Just look at you."

Amanda kept chewing, but Skye could tell she was embarrassed.

> ☆❋ SOME THINGS ABOUT ❋☆
> MELISSA and TAYLOR,
> the BAD BALLERINAS
>
> 1. They are like the food police here.
> 2. In fact, just about all they think about is food.
> 3. And clothes.
> 4. And boys.
> 5. They hardly ever laugh—or even smile.
> 6. But it is fun to spy on them.
> 7. And they are probably VERY GOOD DANCERS.

Pip cleared his throat. "Hey, Del Vecchio, do you know how much sugar is in that yogurt you're carrying around?"

"It's fat-free, stupid," Melissa said, cradling the little container to her chest as if protecting it from Pip's sarcasm. Aaron Petterson and Taylor Shusterman—the other bad ballerina—came up behind her, curious to see what was happening, with Danko, Cord, and Kee slouching close behind. Kee looked apprehensive, which made Skye like him a little bit more.

"Yeah, but how much *sugar?*" Pip asked, not backing down.

Aaron started prancing around, flapping his hands. *"How much sugar? How much sugar?"* he said, doing his version of a sissy voice, and a bunch of kids sitting nearby started laughing.

"Everyone knows yogurt is good for you, *Philip,*" Taylor said with a sniff, coming to Melissa's defense. She tugged at her pink top, which was cropped as high as the belly-button police at Amelia Earhart would allow.

"Pipsqueak. Pansy," Aaron said to Pip—*again*. It was kind of like his refrain.

"He is not a pansy," Amanda peeped in her helium voice, having finally swallowed her bite of sandwich. "And anyway, it's really bad to call people names like that. It's prob'ly even against the law. It's like a hate crime, practically!"

"Oh," Aaron said, looking mean and happy at the same

**Fun at Lunch
(Part Two)**   · 74 ·

time. "The pipsqueak pansy's fat little friend is sticking up for him! And what makes you the expert about whether or not Pip is a—?" Aaron mouthed the insult and waggled his hands in the air again.

"Shut up," Amanda and Pip said in unison.

"And Amanda's not fat," Skye heard herself say. Maddy nudged her ribs.

"C'mon," Danko said to Aaron, bored. "Let's book. Who cares who's gay?"

"I'm not gay!" Pip shouted, and for some reason, his voice rang out loud and clear above the surrounding din as if he were making an announcement over the intercom. Nearly every head turned, and kids pointed and laughed.

Aaron smirked. *"Now* we can book," he announced happily.

"I'm ruined," Pip muttered twenty minutes later in art class as they worked on their self-portraits. "Everyone heard me say it. I hate those guys!"

"I didn't hear," Matteo whispered, trying to make him feel better. "I was eating outside. I heard about it later, though," he confessed. "I said, 'Dude, no way.'"

"Thanks, I *guess*," Pip told him. His freckles seemed to be standing out more than usual on his face, which was pale, Skye noticed.

"Well, he called me fat," Amanda said, "but *I* don't

care. I'm not ruined. I hate him, too, though."

"Excuse me, people," Ms. O'Hare called out, looking up from the art book she was studying. "But I don't think self-portraits call for a whole lot of chitchat. I'll be coming around in five minutes for individual critiques, so please get to work."

Skye bent over her assignment—which was a lot more interesting than what they'd been doing in art activities

Self-Portraits in Art Class

lately. In art activities, they'd been toiling away on posters for the food drive, and on a banner for November's Homecoming game, and on posters for the dance, which was called "The Turkey Trot," for some crazy reason, and on the special Homecoming newspaper, which promised to be dull beyond belief.

"Guess what?" Amanda whispered. "My mom says I can give a costume party the Saturday before Halloween, and all the art activity kids can come. Maddy, too, if she wants," she told Skye. "But don't tell anyone else about the party, you guys," she added as Ms. O'Hare came gliding toward their table. It's just gonna be us art jerks, that's all. But it'll be fun!"

(⑤)

Dear Scott, Things are okay at school, but the 8th grade kids I told you about have gotten worse. They keep picking on us art jerks for no reason. (Well, not on me, exactly, but mostly Aaron picks on Pip, who he calls gay and queer.)

I never know what to do when someone is mean to someone else. I mean, if I say something, will the mean person be mean to me next? And if I don't say anything, doesn't that make me mean, too? (You used to be kind of mean to me. Remember the sleepover party you wrecked? And that time at the restaurant?? And, and, and???)

Here is a mystery: a secret drawing got slipped into my locker! Oh, and Gran had another date. How totally embarrassing! Love, Skye

(⑤)

HI SKYE. I DONT REMBER BEING MEAN 2 YOU, JUST MOM + DAD. WELL A COUPLE TIMES 2 YOU MABE. SORRY. I DONT

KNOW WHY I ACT THE WAY I DID, I CANT REMBER. BUT I
REMBER BENG NORMAL 4 SOME RESON I WISH I DIDNT. ON
HALLWEEN ME AND MOM GO 2 THE MOVIES 4 A TRET. NOW
THAT IS PATHTIC. DAD STAY HOME ANSER THE DOOR SO I
DONT SCARE ANY KIDS HAHA. IF I WAS IN CALFORNA THEY
LEAVE PIP ALONE 4 GOOD. THIS ONE GUY AT MY SCHOL 2
YRS AGO KEEPS CALLING GUYS GAY AND IT TURNS OUT
HE WAS THE ONE!!! HE CAME OUT LATER HE WAS NICE
AFTR THAT, EVEN COOL. SAY HI 2 GRAN, MABE SHE TAKES
YOU ON HER DATE!!!! NOW THATS SCARY. LOVE, SCOTT

12

Remembering

"**D**o you remember that Thanksgiving, the time I visited you in Albuquerque?" Gran asked the next Saturday afternoon, steam from her tea misting her glasses as she and Skye watched an old movie on TV. "You were what, eight years old? Nine?"

Skye didn't really remember much about the visit—except for some weird dinners when Gran tried to "*help out*" in the kitchen, almost driving Skye's mom nuts in the process. "Mmm-hmm," she said, listening to the rain. "That was the year Scott threw the bowl of cranberry sauce on the floor because it wasn't from a can."

Gran winced a little, newly remembering. "Scotty always was a handful, wasn't he?" she acknowledged reluctantly. "I still have pictures of that trip somewhere," she added, looking around, as if they might be tucked away under a nearby sofa cushion. And then she sighed—probably thinking about Scott now, Skye thought. "I remember when you were born, Skye," Gran said softly. "I was teasing Scotty over the phone, asking if you were a boy or a girl, and he said, 'It's just a baby, Gran. And I'm gonna help take care of it.' Fierce as could be. And from that moment on, he was always looking out for you."

Skye nodded politely and sipped her hot chocolate. "*Just a baby.*" She'd seen the pictures, and it was true: she had looked like a red-faced, bleary-eyed blob when she was first born, all wrapped up tight like a burrito, with a little cotton cap jammed down on her wobbly head.

But Scott *had* taken care of her when they were little, Skye remembered suddenly. He'd pulled her around in his Radio Flyer wagon for so many years that someone on another block once asked if there was something wrong with her. "Nope," Scott said angrily. "But she doesn't have to walk as long as I'm here." That was one famous family story, among many others.

Scott was her hero, and she had adored him.

But then, as if he was following instructions from an invisible manual called "How to Make Everyone Miserable," came the impossible years.

Yet their parents had somehow figured Scott would be a good driver?

Why, Skye wondered angrily, had they even allowed Scott to get his license? Was it simply to make their own lives easier? "He'll be able to take you to school," Skye remembered her mom—exhausted even back then—saying just last March. "And maybe this is exactly the show of confidence he needs."

Well, Skye thought sadly, he'd shown *them*.

And so now, instead of her being a little girl relying on her brother to pull her around the neighborhood in his Radio Flyer wagon, she was a girl whose big brother needed *her*. Or he might, someday.

Skye thought about it almost every night: Was it still "two steps forward, one step back" for Scott, as Ms. Santina once put it?

It was impossible to tell without being in Albuquerque, because Scott never talked much in his e-mails about how his rehab was going. And whenever her mom and dad called Sierra Madre, they were obviously trying to stay "focused on the positive," as Skye's dad liked to say.

Gran didn't seem to know how Scott was doing, either,

❀MY BROTHER and ME❀

1. My parents decided to have Scott and me, BUT I never decided to have a brother. IT JUST HAPPENED.
2. So we are stuck with each other.
3. And from now on, Scott will probably always need me more than I need him.

judging by the questions she asked. But then, Skye's mom and dad had always taken pride in not blabbing about their problems—even to family.

But what if Scott stopped moving forward at all? Would she, Skye, have to step in someday and help take care of him?

Skye didn't know how she felt about that. After all, Scott had messed up big-time, while she had always tried to be the *good* kid. So was this going to be her reward?

"Are you cold?" Gran asked Skye, noticing the shiver.

"No, I'm fine," Skye said. "But what made you think of Thanksgiving, Gran?" she asked, as the still-muted movie resumed, following a string of commercials.

"Oh," Gran said, smiling. "It's just a little something I've been dreaming up. You'll find out soon enough, my darling."

13

Trick-or-Treat

~~~~~~

"Happy three-days-before-Halloween," an excited Maddy said as Skye answered the front door. "You look are you supposed to be, like, a girl ninja warrior?" she asked Skye, looking momentarily confused as she adjusted her kitten ears.

Maddy was wearing a pink plush costume that looked like pajamas, if you didn't count the tail, Skye observed, wishing now that she had time to change. She had chosen a costume that was the closest to invisible that she could come up with: scowly dark eyebrows, skinny black pants, a black shirt buttoned all the way up to her neck, and a fake orchid pinned to her chest. Anyone in Albuquerque or Santa Fe would know who she was supposed to be.

"I'm Georgia O'Keeffe," she told Maddy, sounding

grouchy. "She was a famous artist who used to live in New Mexico. She always dressed in black."

"Why?" Maddy asked.

"I don't know," Skye said, irritated by the question. "Because it was easy, I guess. At least her clothes always matched."

"Well, you certainly couldn't go trick-or-treating dressed like that, or you'd get run over," Gran said, bustling into the front hall holding her car keys. "But I guess it's fine for a party. Maddy, you look darling," she said.

Maddy beamed and fiddled with her fuzzy ears again. "I'm really happy I was invited," she said. "This is the best thing that has happened to me since forever."

Skye scowled, still worrying about her costume.

Maddy cocked her head. "You *really* look like a ninja warrior when you make that face, Skye," she said. "Maybe

that's what you should say you are, when we get to Amanda's house, because more people would guess right than if you said you were Georgie Keef."

"*Jor-ja Oh-Keefe*," Skye said, trying not to snap, because it was just plain weird for someone like Maddy—not that Skye meant anything bad by that!—to be so worried and protective about her, Skye McPhee. "Georgia O'Keeffe is extremely well known," Skye said, softening her tone. "She painted orchids and bones and stuff."

"Why?" Maddy asked as Gran locked the front door behind them and they made their way toward the Toyota, Maddy's pink tail swishing against the low bushes that lined Gran's front path. "Why did she do that, Skye?"

"I don't know," Skye said, nearly growling the words. "I really don't want to talk about it."

"Okay, Skye," Maddy said, unperturbed—and prepared to have a wonderful evening—as long as there were no green peppers on any of the food.

At least now I don't feel so bad about ≥MY OWN≤ costume! THANKS, PIP!

As it turned out, Pip was the only other kid who'd even tried for an art-related costume. "Who are you supposed to be?" Maddy asked, eyeing his curly blond wig, his polka-dotted dress, his skinny, twirling-up mustache, the cut-out picture of a clock drooping over one shoulder, and his bulging chest with thinly disguised alarm.

"I'm two people," Pip said proudly. "I'm the surrealist artist Salvador Dalí, and I'm the country singer Dolly Parton. So I'm Salvador Dalí Parton."

"I think Pip's going to win it for both guts and originality," Amanda's mother said, setting down a big box of Halloween decorations on the front porch.

"Skye is Georgie Keef, who was a famous Mexican artist who painted bones," Maddy announced uncertainly.

"*New* Mexican. *New* Mexican," Skye said, trying to be polite as she said the words. But it was hard not to sound snappish. New Mexico was famous, in New Mexico, anyway, and Albuquerque had a population of over half a million! But no one in Sierra Madre even seemed to know that Albuquerque existed, much less that New Mexico was part of the United States.

Duh.

"Oh," Mrs. Berrigan said. "Georgia *O'Keeffe.* Very clever, dear. Now, listen, Amanda," she said over her shoulder as her daughter—masquerading in a drooping tutu and lots of makeup as a bad ballerina, which Skye now wished she'd thought of herself—erupted onto the porch with Jamila and Matteo close behind. "No crepe-paper streamers, because the dew will make them sag by Halloween, which is not until Tuesday," Mrs. Berrigan told them. "But everything else in here should be fine," she said, patting the cardboard box she'd been carrying.

And in no time, phase one of Amanda's party began, and the art jerks were so busy making a scary masterpiece of the Berrigans' front porch that everyone's costume was forgotten, to Skye's intense relief.

"Step back a little farther, Skye, and tell us how it looks," Amanda called from the front porch forty-five minutes later—kind of bossily, Skye thought, but in keeping with her bad ballerina costume. Amanda sounded just like Taylor Shusterman, in fact.

The Berrigans' porch glowed like a stage set as Skye trudged across the wet lawn toward the street,

**Amanda channels Taylor...
Ooo, it's eerie!**

which was dark on this moonless October night. Streetlights in the small foothill town were scarce among the narrow roads that crept rootlike into the canyons.

"It looks good, Amanda," Skye called out as convincingly as she could, though she thought they should have stopped decorating the porch fifteen minutes ago. Now, rubber bats hung from the porch ceiling, the Styrofoam tombstones—illogically dripping with pretend blood—leaned crazily against the light-festooned front door, pumpkins balanced precariously on the porch railing, and spiderweb strands had been tossed in large and unconvincing hunks over absolutely everything. "It looks good," Skye shouted again, wondering when their hamburgers would be ready. Her stomach growled.

"I can barely even hear you—or see you, it's so dark," Amanda yelled back. "Pip's coming out there to check, 'cause I have to go inside and help my mom. Hang on."

"I'm hanging, I'm hanging," Skye muttered to herself. She shifted her feet in the soggy grass as Pip came toward her, his wig jammed low on his head and his temporarily enlarged chest leading the way.

Pip turned and regarded the Berrigans' porch for one long, considering moment. "It looks like a craft store exploded," he finally said. "But Amanda likes it. And I definitely don't wanna have to start again."

"I know," Skye said, laughing. "If we say anything, we'll *never* get to eat."

Pip tilted his head and looked at the porch again. "Maybe you can't go too far this time of year," he said, obviously struggling to turn his artistic opinion around.

"Maybe not," Skye agreed. "So let's tell Amanda it looks fine, and then we can—"

"Boo," a voice behind them said. "Trick-or-treat!"

14

Trouble

Skye whirled around, her heart seeming to leap into her throat, but Pip turned more slowly, as if he knew that the only thing awaiting him was trouble—because the jeering voice had belonged to Aaron Petterson. And looming behind him in the dark were Danko, Cord, and Kee.

"What are you guys doing here?" Skye asked, struggling to keep her voice steady.

"I live a block away," Aaron told her. "Not that it's any of your business." He leaned forward and took a closer look at Skye. "It's that girl from Mexico," he told his friends. "That Skye-chick. And she's gone all retro and Goth for that fat chick's party."

"Skye's from *New* Mexico," Kee said quietly, reluctantly.

"I'm supposed to be Georgia O'Keeffe," Skye heard herself object in a quavering voice. "And Amanda's not fat."

This was just too bizarre, Skye scolded herself instantly—and silently. She could not believe she was

UH-OH

arguing with an eighth-grader about her Halloween costume and Amanda Berrigan's weight, of all things—in temporary Sierra Madre, California, on a cold Saturday night in October. What had happened to her nice, ordinary life in Albuquerque, New Mexico, where the real people lived?

And where were Amanda, Jamila, Matteo, and Maddy? Or Amanda's parents, for that matter? Inside, probably, eating hamburgers and chips, and guzzling soda.

"Whatever," Aaron said, already losing interest. He shifted his attention to Pip, whose identity was still hidden by the darkness, by the blond wig that covered his hair—and by the two large and prominent bumps underneath his polka-dotted dress. The blond hair and the bumps were obviously what had attracted Aaron's attention. "Who's this?" Aaron asked, teasing, and he reached out to lift Pip's chin a little so he could get a better look.

It was obvious to Skye that Aaron thought Pip was a girl—because a guy wouldn't dare touch another guy's face that way.

Pip swatted at Aaron's hand and turned his head, but the unexpected result of this was that Aaron's hand grazed Pip's fake mustache. *"Eee!"* Aaron squealed, jumping back a little. "It's a dude!"

Sometimes I laugh at inappropriate times... ...like now, for instance.

"No way," Cord said. He reached forward, grabbed the end of Pip's mustache, and gave it a tug.

"Give that back," Pip roared, reaching for the twirl of stiffened hair that Cord's paw was now gripping. "I made that!"

"Hey!" Cord shouted, shaking his hand as if Pip's half-mustache was the world's longest centipede. And seeing this, Skye couldn't help but giggle.

"Shut up," Cord yelled at her.

"*'I made that,'*" Aaron Petterson mimicked, concentrating on Pip, and he gave Pip a shove that sent him staggering back a step or two on the Berrigans' lawn.

Skye automatically reached out to grab Pip's arm, but Pip brushed her away. "Leave me alone," he shouted angrily, but Skye couldn't tell whether he was talking to her or to Aaron—and she wasn't about to ask.

"It's the pipsqueak pansy," Aaron shouted, finally recognizing Pip, and he gave Pip another shove, knocking him to the ground.

"Stop *saying* that!" Skye heard herself object loudly.

"He tried to trick us," Cord yelled, furious, and, eager to erase his earlier humiliation, he drew his leg back as if he were about to attempt to kick a field goal. And then— *thud!* Cord's foot connected with Pip's ribs.

"Hey," Danko and Kee objected simultaneously.

"*Uhh,*" Pip groaned as the air was knocked out of him,

and he tried to roll away from the
blows that were sure to follow.

"Stop that!" Skye cried, panicked.

"Quit it, dude. You made your
point," Kee said to Cord, grabbing
his arm and pulling him away
from Pip.

But it was Aaron's leg that
was going back for the kick this
time.

This was really, really happening,
Skye told herself, stunned.

"*Hey*," a man's voice shouted from across the street,
and suddenly, the beam of light from a powerful flashlight
swept across their faces. "What the heck is going on over
there?"

"They—they were beating my friend up for no reason,"
Skye cried, her words tumbling out into the night.

"We were not," Cord said, sounding both innocent and
outraged.

"Yeah," Aaron said. "And I live around here."

The flashlight beam rested on Aaron's face for a
moment. "Oh, it's you," the man said as he approached the
group of kids, his voice flat and unsurprised.

"Hi, Mr. Walters," Aaron said with no change in his
expression. "These kids were making a lot of noise, and we

just stopped by to see if anything was the matter."

"You guys are what's the matter," Skye exclaimed, hoping like crazy she wasn't about to start crying. "We were just standing here! Are you okay, Pip?"

(If I talk fast enough, maybe he'll feel better.)

As Pip struggled to his feet, Skye could make out two orange balloons—Pip's former Dolly Parton chest, she supposed—bouncing across the lawn like escaping ghosts. "I'm fine," Pip said. He tried to stand up straight, but Skye could tell by the way he clutched his side that he was in pain.

"Are you okay, son?" the man with the flashlight asked, echoing Skye.

"I'm fine," Pip said again.

"See?" Aaron said to the man—in a tone of voice that was just this side of rude, in Skye's opinion. "Everything's great."

"Let's go," Kee murmured, taking a few steps back, and Danko and Cord stepped back, too. But Aaron didn't move.

"I'll be keeping my eye on you, Mr. Petterson," the man said to Aaron. "C'mon, kids," he said, turning to Pip and Skye. "I'll walk you to the Berrigans' front door."

"Buh-bye," Aaron called out after them, his voice fake-nice, cheerful, and threatening—all at the same time. "See you guys at school!"

So much for being invisible, Skye thought, resigned to whatever was going to happen next.

15

Revenge!

HI SKYE, HOW WAS THE PARTY LAST WKND? MOM AND
DAD GO 2 CONSELING NOW THEY YELL ALOT, EVEN MORE
THAN BEFOR. I HAF 2 STAYE IN THE WATING RM IT SUX BUT
IT IS BETTR THAN A BABYSITR. JERMY CAME OVER IT WAS
COOL AT FRST BUT WE RAN OUT OF STUFF TO SAY IT WS
WERD. I WANT 2 MOVE AWAY FRM HERE. LOVE SCOTT

Dear Scott, I am freaking out about Mom and Dad going in for
counseling! They are fighting even <u>more</u>?? Doesn't our family
have enough problems??? That is so irresponsible of them!!!!

    I'm sorry you and Jeremy ran out of stuff to say to each
other when he came over. It must have felt so strange, not that
you guys ever used to talk all that much, as I recall. Not like me
and Hana, who never e-mails me at all anymore, by the way.

It's Only Temporary

I am afraid things will just keep getting worse and worse
for us art jerks. Those football guys basically crashed Amanda's
party last weekend and beat up Pip, or at least they tried to—all
because of his costume, which was really out there. But he
was only trying to be super-crazy and make Amanda laugh and
notice him.

Love, Skye

P.S. Guess what? I got a second mystery drawing in my locker,
and I think I know who did it! (But I'm not 100% sure. . . .)

Pip thinks we should get even, but...

"We gotta think of some way to get even with them, or they're gonna keep going after us," Pip said the following Thursday afternoon when Ms. O'Hare left the art activities room to take some papers to the office. "They think we're easy targets."

"Oh, no," Maddy murmured, her face losing its color. She was obviously imagining another so-called "collision," Skye thought, biting her lip in sympathy.

She didn't know what to fear for herself.

Ms. O'Hare's art activities group had started meeting on Thursdays as well as Tuesdays, because work was piling up. Homecoming was in two more weeks, and there was still the thirty-foot-long banner to finish and the special Homecoming newspaper to assemble. "Amelia Earhart is gonna kick Thomas Alva Edison's *butt* this year," Aaron and his friends kept going around saying, to Skye's secret delight.

Matteo Molina shifted in his seat. "I dunno," he mumbled. "What can we do?"

"I didn't even tell my dad what happened at the party," Pip said. "He'd probably say it was my own fault for taking art. He says art is for girls. You better believe I had to sneak my Halloween costume out of the house that night!"

"I used to get that, too—about art," Matteo confirmed. "Until my uncle got a job in computer graphics and started making more money than anyone else in the family."

"The grown-ups at school don't really care about what happens away from school," Amanda informed everyone, "so you can't tell *them* when something goes wrong. But bad stuff is going to keep on happening—at both places. To *us*."

"I don't get why those football guys even care about us," Skye said, shaking her head. "When my brother was in middle school, he and his friends never paid attention to any younger kids. They were too busy messing around and stuff."

"I didn't know you had a brother, Skye," Maddy said, her brown eyes widening in surprise. "Why didn't you ever tell me that?"

Because Scott was one of *her* syndromes, that was why, Skye thought, not meeting Maddy's curious gaze.

"Well," Amanda said, ignoring both the subject of Skye's brother and Maddy's question, "I don't know why they're picking on us. Maybe they're bored, or maybe they just hate anyone who's different from them."

Scott and Maddy, Skye thought immediately. They were different, too, and they always would be, at least a little, and people would judge them—and maybe even be mean to them—*because* they were different.

And it wasn't a temporary thing for them.

"I can do something about it," she heard herself say.

All the art kids looked at her in silence for a second. "Yeah, right," Pip finally said, laughing.

"No, I mean it," Skye told him—and the others. "I can. Because we're in charge of the Homecoming newspaper they're giving out at half-time, right?"

A couple of the kids nodded.

"Well, you know that insert that's going to be inside the newspaper?" Skye asked. "The one with all the football players' individual pictures in it?"

"Yes," Amanda said cautiously. "I heard everyone gets the players to sign the pictures, and then

I can hear myself talking, but I can't shut up. Someone STOP ME!

kids tape them inside their lockers—as if those guys were rock stars!"

"Like they aren't getting enough attention already," Pip said, outraged.

"And the school might even put the insert in the yearbook this year—for the very first time," Jamila reported.

"Not when I get done with it, they won't," Skye said. "'Cause I'm gonna do a job on the mean guys' pictures. You know, fix them up a little—or draw whole new ones and sneak them in. I mean, those guys are messing with us because they think we don't have any way of getting back at them, right? So this'll teach them a lesson."

"You could do that?" Matteo asked, sounding skeptical.

"Yeah, like what are you gonna do?" Jamila chimed in. "Draw mustaches on their pictures? 'Cause that's just lame."

"I can do better than that," Skye said, sliding her sketchbook out of her book bag. Her heart was pounding as she mentally reviewed the drawings inside it: there were those really mean drawings of Scott she'd done last summer when she was still so angry with him, not that any of these kids knew Scott. But there was also that drawing of Pip that made him look freakishly flexible and thin, like some kind of mutant, and the one of Jamila wearing the world's goofiest smile, and the one that made Matteo look like a sumo wrestler on a bad day, and the one of

Amanda that made her look like she was made entirely out of twisted party balloons.

And then there was the drawing of Maddy—made just a week after Skye had arrived in Sierra Madre—that made her look completely out of it, as if her brain was totally empty. That drawing would hurt the most, Skye knew, suddenly ashamed. You could draw a bad picture of anyone, really—especially when you didn't know them.

"Let me show you a couple of drawings, just so you can get the idea," Skye said. "But you have to back up a little, 'cause this is private. It's like my journal." She hurriedly selected a few harmless pages to show them, and the art kids were quiet for a moment.

"Hey, those are pretty good," Amanda said, surprised.

"They're *really* good," Matteo said, leaning in close to get a better look. "But do you think you could draw those actual guys? So people could recognize them, I mean?"

Skye nodded. "I can try," she said. "I'll just make 'em look a little more . . . *interesting*."

"Great!" Pip said, looking hopeful for the first time all day. "Revenge! This could really, really work, Skye—if you can make those guys look bad in front of everyone. We'll teach 'em what happens when they mess with us art jerks."

"Teach who not to mess with whom?" Ms. O'Hare said

as she backed into the room holding a cookie sheet.

"Oh, nothing," Amanda, Matteo, and Pip said in unison.

"Well, I made you some quesadillas on the hot-plate in the teachers' lounge," Ms. O'Hare said, grinning, "because I know how hungry you kids get after school. But use plenty of paper towels when you clean up, okay? Because we don't want to leave any fingerprints on anything."

"We'll try not to leave fingerprints," Pip promised, and all the art jerks knew exactly what he was talking about.

But Skye had the distinct and suddenly sinking feeling the only "fingerprints" on this stunt were going to be hers.

Dear Scott, Help!!! I got carried away and came up with a way to get even with the football guys, only I'm probably going to get in trouble for it. But I have to do it! Maddy thinks I definitely will get in trouble, but she says she will back me up, no matter what. That's Maddy.

I wish you were here to give me some advice. Remember

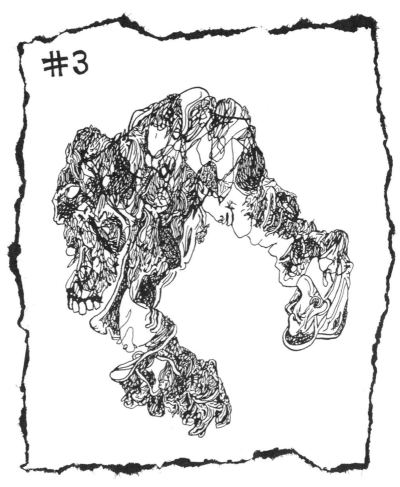

the good old days when we were kids? Remember your Radio
Flyer wagon?? I could use another ride in it about now.
Love, Skye

P.S. Mystery drawing number three! It has teeth at one end
and what looks like a mouth at the other end. What do you
think? Is someone trying to tell me something?

#3

16

Special Edition

~~~~~

Pip strode into the almost empty art activities room ten minutes after school ended, as the muffled *thump thump* of the school band's drums floated in from the playing field. The game was about to begin, and the special edition of the Homecoming newspaper he'd just turned in to the parent volunteers would be given out at halftime.

Skye planned to be long gone by then.

"Did you do it?" Amanda asked in her squeaky voice. "Did they notice anything was wrong with the insert?"

Pip shook his head. "It's not like they would," he told the nervous group of kids. "It's on the inside, and Skye only changed four little pictures. Besides, everyone is gonna be too busy watching the game to check out the paper for at least another hour. It's not like they think anything in it is really *news*."

Pip tells us we pulled it off, but...

"Those guys are going to be so sorry," Amanda whispered, narrowing her eyes in gleeful anticipation. "This'll teach them to be mean to us for no reason."

"And it's not like they didn't already get a lot of attention today," Pip chimed in. "I mean, when is Amelia Earhart ever gonna have a special assembly just for artists? When are *we* going to get to walk across the stage while everyone whistles and claps? And we're the ones with talent. All they ever did was *grow*."

"I've never heard of anyone clapping for artists," Jamila said, frowning. "Even other artists don't clap for artists, I don't think."

It's Only Temporary

"I wonder what Ms. O'Hare is going to say?" Skye asked, her voice tight with sudden worry—because Skye really liked Ms. O'Hare. She was like a cross between an actual artist, a cool older sister, a hippie aunt, and a grown-up friend.

"Where is Ms. O'Hare, anyway?" Maddy asked, looking around nervously, as if their art teacher might suddenly materialize next to the cutting board or near the giant roll of butcher paper.

"She's at the game," Pip said, shrugging. "I guess she loves football."

"I need to go home," Skye announced, trying to keep her voice steady. "Gran's expecting me."

"I'm going with you," Maddy said.

"Well, okay," Pip told them. "But you guys have to come to the Homecoming dance tonight, because we can't act like we're scared of what's gonna happen after Aaron and the other guys see the paper. We gotta see this thing through."

"Ooh," Amanda said under her breath.

"I am kind of scared," Skye admitted, stunned that she

hadn't thought past that triumphant moment when the mean football guys opened the Homecoming paper at half-time in their locker room and saw those drawings they—*she*—had done of them. When they saw how the art jerks had taken their revenge.

But Skye did feel a little bad about having included Kee—maybe-nice Kee? secret artist Kee?—in that act of revenge, she realized suddenly. Because what had Kee done, except to choose the wrong friends?

But that in itself was a pretty dumb thing to do. Just look at Scott.

"I'm scared, too," Maddy announced. "I'm *extremely* scared."

"But you guys are gonna be at the dance, right?" Pip asked everyone again. "We can't hide out forever. We have to get this over with."

"I'll be there," Skye said, nodding reluctantly.

"Well, my mother said I *can't* go to the dance," Maddy said, sounding matter-of-fact and more than a little relieved. "She says it isn't appropriate for sixth-graders to go to the same dance as eighth-grade kids, because of the differences in their levels of development."

The art jerks digested this starchy and complicated bit of news in silence.

"But Amelia Earhart is too poor to put on three separate dances," Amanda told everyone. "I know, 'cause my mom's on the PTA committee. But that's why even the older kids aren't supposed to bring dates. *'It's not that kind of party,'* quote unquote. It's just supposed to be everybody getting together and having fun."

"Ha," Pip said.

"Well," Jamila reported, "my mama says I'm not allowed to go to the dance, either, and I don't even care. All that sweating and grinding! I don't *think* so."

"My mom says grinding's not going to be allowed at Amelia Earhart," Amanda assured Jamila solemnly. "Kids will have to keep at least one balloon distance apart while they dance. But I'm gonna try to have fun," she added, her eyes shining.

"Me, too," Pip said, sliding her a look.

"Me three," Matteo chimed in.

"Well, Maddy and I have to leave," Skye told everyone, since they clearly weren't getting anywhere with this conversation. "So, bye." She looked around the art activities room, wondering if there was something she was forgetting. This had been the craziest day ever.

"Come on, Skye," Maddy told her, uncharacteristically impatient. "My mother doesn't like to be kept waiting for extended periods of time."

"See you tonight," Amanda said to Skye.

"Let's meet here in front of the cafeteria, okay?" Pip suggested. "At seven thirty? So we can walk into the gym together?" He sounded nervous for the first time.

"Okay," Skye said, feeling sorry for him—and for herself too, she supposed numbly, because who knew what was going to happen at that dance?

She was probably just frazzled, Skye told herself, but she kept thinking she was forgetting something. . . .

But Pip was right, she knew; they had to see this through. They had to get it over with. "C'mon, Maddy," she said softly. "Let's go home."

17

Butterflies

"We're going the wrong way," Maddy observed as they walked east, rather than west, along Grandview Avenue. "I don't want my mother to start worrying."

"I just want to spy on the game for a minute," Skye said, heading for the chain-link fence that separated Amelia Earhart's playing field from the street.

A school bus—for the Thomas Alva Edison football team, Skye figured—was parked next to the curb, and parents' cars were crammed closely together, filling all the rest of the available parking spaces.

This game really *was* a big deal, Skye realized, looking through the chain link at the crowd of people that had assembled, and new butterflies fluttered in her stomach. "Squeeze in between the bus and the Audi," she whispered to Maddy, as though the noisy throng of people far across the field somehow might otherwise hear her.

"Okay," Maddy said, crowding in close behind Skye. "But I don't know what we're looking for."

Neither did Skye, for that matter, but she had never been to a middle-school football game before, and she was curious.

Amelia Earhart's all-purpose playing field had been spruced up for this occasion, with colorful bunches of balloons everywhere. The field had only one long stretch of bleachers, on the other side of the field, and half the seats were filled with Thomas Alva Edison boosters, while the other half was jammed with Amelia Earhart fans.

The school band milled around one end of the bleachers—getting ready for halftime, Skye guessed, which was also when the newspaper would be given out. Assorted practice drum rolls and horn bleats floated their way across the field, over the heads of the players, who seemed to be waiting for a decision to be made toward one end of the field while their coaches stalked back and forth like outraged flamingos along the sidelines, and competing cheerleaders shook their pom-poms in each others' direction.

The panorama stretched in front of Skye and Maddy like a movie scene. The football players looked kind of small from where she and Maddy were lurking, Skye thought, almost feeling sorry for them.

But no, the guys who'd been bullying them deserved

what was going to happen, she told herself sternly. And anyway, it was too late to change things now.

At the opposite side of the field, in front of the bleachers, were strung a few long benches where the extra football players sat, though a few players in front of the benches were stretching and running in place like windup toys.

And behind them sat Aaron, Cord, Danko, and Kee, helmets in their laps. Although she was staring across the width of the field, Skye could see them as clear as anything. It was as though her vision was suddenly super-powerful.

"That's the offense sitting on the bench," Maddy informed her. "I guess Thomas Alva Edison is about to score, that's what the problem is. Our defense is trying to stop them."

"How do you know all that?" Skye asked, astonished, turning halfway around to stare at her friend.

Maddy shrugged. "I watch a lot of football with my dad," she explained. "It's a very interesting game."

Skye turned her gaze back to the field—and then the butterflies stopped fluttering for a moment. "Oh, no," she whispered.

"What?" Maddy whispered back.

"They're handing out the newspaper *now*," Skye said. "To the players on the sidelines, anyway. Too early! Too early!"

And the scene unfolded in what seemed to Skye like

slow motion: the floppy stack of newspapers—complete with inserts—made its way down the football players' benches. Win or lose, receiving this newspaper—getting this *honor*—was supposed to be the players' supreme moment of glory, Skye realized, suddenly feeling sick.

The Amelia Earhart players—including Aaron, Cord, Danko, and Kee—opened the papers casually, not wanting to seem too eager to see their own faces.

Amelia Earhart Middle School is counting on you!

Danko Marshall

Aaron Petterson

Cord Driscoll

Kee Williams

And then the guffaws rippled up and down the benches as other players saw the insert for the first time. Many of the boys got to their feet, trying to catch a glimpse of the look on the faces of the four players Skye had drawn.

And in spite of how far away she stood, Skye could see Aaron's head bend low over the opened paper as if he couldn't believe his eyes.

Cord threw the paper onto the grass in front of him, disgusted.

Danko sat perfectly still, staring at the ground.

And Kee seemed to be looking straight across the field at Maddy and Skye.

He couldn't actually see them, could he?

"Quick," Skye told Maddy. "Behind the bus!"

"But then we'll be in the street," Maddy pointed out, her brown eyes wide with alarm. "And we could get run over."

"Just do it," Skye cried, and the two girls virtually oozed around the bus in their attempt to escaped Kee's steady gaze.

Skye peeked around the corner of the bus one last time. The crowd in the bleachers was murmuring now like a single giant beast, curious about what was happening down on the sidelines—but the fistfuls of newspapers now being handed out in the stands soon filled everyone in.

Skye could hear the laughter build from where she stood.
And Aaron, Cord, Danko, and Kee just sat there.

⑥

**Dear Scott, Well, I drew the cartoons of those football guys,
and we sneaked them into the newspaper, all right. Now
everyone has seen them. And it's hard to explain, but I feel
really bad about the whole thing.**

    But tonight I have to go to that dance. I have no choice.

    **(One of the boys I drew—Kee Williams—is probably the
mystery artist! And maybe he's not so bad, after all. But I
can't turn back the clock.)**

    **I can't believe this is happening to me! Wish me luck
tonight. Love, Skye**

⑥

**HI SKYE, WE ARE ONLIN AT THE SAME TIME, HAHAHA!
ONLY I AM WORRIT ABOT THAT DANCE, YOU SHOUD
TELL GRAN MABE OR JUST STAY HOME. WHY DO U
HAVE 2 GO??? U ALWAS HAVE A CHOCE. ALMOST ALWAS
ANYWAYS. WRITE ME WHEN U GET BACK I WILL WATE UP
2 HEAR. I HATE THOSE GUYS EVEN KEE LOVE SCOTT**

18

The Turkey Trot

"You look absolutely adorable, Skye," Gran said, beaming her approval.

"Thanks," Skye said, fidgeting with the square neckline of the one dress she'd brought with her to Sierra Madre.

"You're going to have the greatest time," Gran promised.

"If you say so," Skye said, trying not to sound too gloomy.

"You seem to have made lots of new friends at Amelia Earhart," Gran pointed out, sticking to the McPhee family tradition of focusing on the positive, no matter what. "You'll have to invite them over sometime," she added, smiling.

"Yeah," Skye teased. "We can have a tofu party."

"I've eased up," Gran protested. "Admit it."

It was true, Skye thought; last weekend, Gran had even

Gran and I are getting used to each other,
and Sierra Madre is starting to feel like home.
(But don't tell anyone!)

gone so far as to buy chips—multigrain, salt-free, and baked, not fried, of course—and soda, or some fruity drink a little *like* soda.

"Okay, I admit it," Skye said, looking at the living-room clock. "But we'd better get going, Gran, 'cause I'm supposed to meet up with my friends exactly twelve minutes from now."

"Oh, no," Gran said, her eyes wide as she checked the clock's time against her wristwatch. "That clock's running fifteen minutes slow, Skye. It must need winding."

"It's *slow*?" Skye exclaimed, squawking the two words. "Hurry up, Gran—or I'm gonna have to walk into that stupid dance all by myself!"

x

Skye hesitated alone near the wide-open gymnasium doors, wishing she'd asked Gran to turn the Toyota around and take her straight back to Eucalyptus Terrace. Her fellow art jerks must already be thinking she'd decided to stay home; they sure weren't waiting for her in front of the cafeteria, the way Pip said they would be.

I never even had a NIGHTMARE this bad.

The inside of the school gymnasium looked golden from where Skye was standing. Under the big wall clock at the end of the room was the banner the art activities kids had made saying "We Won!" but someone had had to add a small, red, last-minute "Almost," just between the "We" and the "Won."

Uh-oh, Skye thought, taking a step back. Amelia Earhart had lost the Homecoming game to Thomas Alva Edison. This was not good.

"Come on in, honey," a committee mom said, peeking out from the doorway. "Don't be shy about being here alone. It's not that kind of party."

"I know," Skye said, taking another step back. "I heard."

"*There* you are," Amanda said, popping out from behind the woman.

"Finally," Pip and Matteo chorused. They appeared to be attached to Amanda's side by invisible strips of Velcro, and when they dragged Skye into the gymnasium, she joined the cluster.

"Have you seen them yet?" Skye asked, shouting to be heard above the voices and music that swirled around them. "What's happening?"

"I don't know," Pip said, sounding both excited and scared. "Everyone's talking about the drawings, though. We did it!"

"Hey, Skye-chick," a voice said, and then she heard the art jerks inhale as if they were one person.

Skye turned around. "Hey," she said cautiously, seeing Aaron, Cord, Danko, Kee, and the two bad ballerinas standing in front of her, their toes turned out as usual. Kee looked troubled, staring down at the scuffed gymnasium floor as if there were a message hidden there.

"So, you think you're, like, this really hot artist, huh?" Aaron asked Skye, sneering. "Making us lose the game."

"You are so gonna get it," Taylor told Skye, and she smiled—though it was not a pretty sight.

Skye could not think of what to say, because—how had they known so quickly that she was the one who had done those drawings? And how had she made them lose the game?

And, most important of all, how was she "gonna get it?"

Taylor says I'm gonna get it, but I think I already got it. And I'm SICK of it!

"Skye's drawings are great," Pip said, trying to defend her. "They looked more like you guys than your team photos did, that's for sure."

"Shut up, pansy," Aaron said, not looking at him.

"Stop *saying* that," Amanda told him, but this time she could barely squeak out her objection, she was so scared.

"I was talking to Skye-chick, here," Aaron said. "We got something to show her."

Melissa nudged Taylor. They looked excited, and they both stared at Skye with hungry eyes.

"What?" Skye asked, in spite of herself.

"C'mon," Aaron said, laughing. "It's over by the clock. Come see for yourself!"

"And bring your pathetic little posse," Melissa added.

The two groups shuffled over toward the big wall clock, threading their way through the mob of laughing, dancing kids, who seemed oblivious to this new drama that was unfolding. "At least we're in a public place," Pip muttered.

"Yeah," Amanda squeaked. "He can't actually *hurt* Skye. But I wish I'd stayed home," she added softly. "I'm scared!"

"Skye's the one who should be scared," Matteo pointed out, sounding matter-of-fact—and even a little relieved, Skye thought. Not that she blamed Matteo for feeling that way.

"Up there," Aaron said. "Whaddya think, Skye-chick? How do you like it?"

Skye forced herself to raise her eyes to where Aaron was pointing.

High above her head, drawings of Pip, Amanda, Matteo, Jamila, and Maddy were taped to the wall.

They weren't anywhere near the worst ones of them she had done. In fact, they were kind of okay. But—

"Skye did those," a surprised Amanda announced to no one in particular.

"Yeah, and there are plenty more where they came

from," Aaron said in a threatening way, as if reading Skye's thoughts. "Skye knows what I mean. Just wait."

Kee cleared his throat; he looked embarrassed, Skye thought dully.

"The custodian let us into the art room after the game," Cord said, grinning. "Aaron told him he'd left something important in there."

"Too bad about that lame-o retarded brother of yours back in Mexico," Aaron said, watching Skye closely to see—and enjoy—her reaction.

They had her sketchbook.

Dear Scott, You can go to bed now, because I am safe and sound back at Gran's house, and the dance is over. I hate those guys, too, even Kee—more than ever, in fact, because somehow, they got into the art activities room after the game to find out who did those drawings of them, and they took something of mine that I accidentally left there. (Oops.) Love, Skye

19

After the Dance

"Oops."

That was putting it mildly, Skye thought dully the morning after the dance as she lay in bed, pretending to be asleep long past the time Gran usually roused her. Skye was almost more miserable than she had been in her

I am never, never, never, never, never, never, never, never, never getting out of bed again.

(And neither is Señor Monkey.)

entire life. This was right up there with that phone call after Scott's accident.

Back then, she had been miserable mixed with angry, Skye confessed silently.

This was something else altogether. This was miserable mixed with—what?

Embarrassment. Dread. *Loss.*

Skye couldn't stand thinking about the loss of her beloved sketchbook—the last in what had been a whole series of losses. The thought of her own private sketchbook—her *sketchbook!*—being in the hands of the mean football guys and the bad ballerinas—sneering Melissa! patronizing Taylor!—made Skye want to curl up and die.

WHAT WAS IN MY SECRET ❊❋SKETCHBOOK❋❊

1. Grouchy private stuff about Scott.
2. And Mom + Dad.
3. Hurt-feelings stuff about Hana, who I really miss.
4. Sarcastic stuff about Maddy, who I really like.
5. Stuff about how dumb California is compared to New Mexico.
6. Drawings of EVERYONE, and some of them are a little —uh— EXTREME.
7. And my lists!!!

uhhhhhhhhhhhhhhhhhhhhhhh......

What were they doing with the sketchbook right now, besides prying into her innermost feelings and reading about her problems? Laughing at her? Passing around the pages? Or ripping *out* the pages, more likely, getting her drawings photocopied so they could plaster them all over the school on Monday morning?

Skye felt her face grow hot at the very idea of everyone—especially her new friends, and Ms. O'Hare—seeing the worst of those drawings. Ms. O'Hare, Amanda, Jamila, Pip, Matteo, and Maddy—especially Maddy—would be so hurt.

And she really, really liked them all now.

Skye felt like throwing up, only she didn't have the energy to get out of bed.

What she wanted most was to run back home to Albuquerque—only there *wasn't* much home there now. Her house was in an unrecognizable uproar, her parents were fighting more than ever, her brother was changed—maybe forever—and her best friend apparently had forgotten all about her.

"Skye?" Gran asked, rapping gently on Skye's bedroom door. "It's time to get up, darling. It's ten thirty."

"Five more minutes," Skye begged. That usually worked, except on schooldays.

"I know you had a wonderful time last night," Gran said, insistent, "but rise and shine."

"Please," Skye mumbled from under her covers. "I didn't have a wonderful time last night. It was the worst night of my life."

Gran was instantly at Skye's side. She plopped down on the bed and gently pried open one of her granddaughter's squinched-shut eyes. "Talk," she said. "What happened?"

"Nothing," Skye said, turning her head to the wall.

"Talk," Gran said again, but it sounded more like an order this time. "It's important that you tell me what's troubling you, darling. I never had a daughter, but I know this much, at least."

"I can't. It's too terrible," Skye said to the wall.

Instantly, she could feel her grandmother stiffen as she probably imagined all kinds of hideous *Law & Order*–type things happening at the dance, Skye realized, guilt-stricken. "Don't worry, I'm okay," she reassured Gran hastily. "It's just that—some kids stole my sketchbook."

"Your *sketchbook*?" Gran said, unable to hide her relief.

"See, you didn't even know I had one, did you?" Skye said, sitting upright in bed. "And, it's, like the most important thing in my life! It's the only thing I have any control over, anyway. And now it's *gone*. *Worse* than gone."

"How could it be worse than gone?" Gran asked, puzzled.

"Those kids are gonna use it against me," Skye explained softly. "Just to hurt my new friends' feelings, and make them hate me."

"But—why would anyone do such a thing?" Gran asked. "And how could they do it? What's *in* your sketchbook, for heaven's sake?"

"Private stuff I wrote," Skye whispered. "And drawings. And some of them are not-so-nice drawings, too, 'cause I was so mad about everything at first."

"Such as?" Gran asked, smoothing Skye's tangled hair back from her face.

"Such as Scott being so stupid and having that accident," Skye said, shrugging away Gran's hand. "And about Mom and Dad fighting all the time, and then making me move here. No offense," she added.

"None taken," Gran said, smiling a little. "Go on."

"Well, if that's not bad enough, I lost all my Albuquerque friends, too," Skye continued. "Especially Hana, who never even writes me anymore. And I lost the chance to start middle school with all the kids I grew up with! But I could always draw, at least. Nobody could take that away—until now."

"So you lost a sketchbook full of private writings and hurtful drawings that you did because you felt so angry and helpless," Gran said, trying to summarize.

"They aren't *all* hurtful," Skye said. "Just the early

ones. The drawings got nicer once I got to know everyone a little better."

Even Scott, she thought—and that had been the biggest surprise of all.

"It's kind of like everyone I met here became more real to me each time I drew them," Skye tried to explain. "Even the bad kids, in a way."

"So there are nice drawings, too," Gran said, attempting to focus on the positive, McPhee-style.

"Yeah, but my new friends will never know that," Skye said, shaking her head. "Because these kids are probably gonna plaster the school with the *terrible* drawings. And I'll lose all my new friends, and even worse, hurt their feelings. And *they* probably all have syndromes, too. Just like Maddy and me."

"But Skye," Gran said, "I don't understand. Forget the 'syndromes' for a minute, whatever in the world you're talking about *there*. Why do these kids have it in for you? What did you ever do to them?"

Uh-oh, Skye thought, *here we go*. "I—I guess I kind of hurt some of their feelings yesterday," she admitted, unable to look her grandmother in the eye. "Not by accident, exactly, but—I just got carried away. See, me and my friends were trying to get even with those kids for picking on us all the time, so I drew girly pictures of four of the football players, and we sneaked them into the Homecoming newspaper. And everyone saw them at the game."

"Oh, dear," Gran said to herself, before turning back to Skye. "So, taking the sketchbook was these kids' way of getting even?" she asked.

"I guess," Skye said, unable to look at her.

"Hmm. There's a whole lot of getting even going on," Gran observed. "But none of it has worked, has it?"

"And now I'm gonna have to *move*," Skye said, following her own train of thought. "Just when I was thinking about maybe staying here in Sierra Madre the whole year!"

"Staying here, with me?" Gran asked, astonished.

"Don't bother saying no, or anything," Skye mumbled.

REASONS TO STAY WITH
GRAN
IF I GET A CHOICE

1. My gritting-my-teeth headaches are gone!
2. And I'm doing better in school, too.
3. Also, I don't have to listen to my parents FIGHT.
4. And I'm getting to know Scott better, too!
5. Not to mention GRAN.
6. PEACE + QUIET.

"You don't even *have* to. I didn't really mean it. I know I'd just get in your way."

"Darling, you never get in my way," Gran said, shaking her head. "You're just about the best thing that's ever happened to me. Why, you're better than vitamin B!"

Hope flared for Skye, then died in almost the same moment. "But I can't stay," she said softly. "Because of hurting all my new friends' feelings next week. They'll hate me too much."

"Well," Gran said, "you're just going to have to do something about that, aren't you? And no, I don't really have any suggestions. But you'll come up with something."

"I don't think so, Gran," Skye said sadly.

Gran leaned over and planted a warm kiss on Skye's tear-stained cheek. "Up you get," she told Skye. "That's always the first step, my darling. And then hop into a nice hot shower, then we'll get some protein into you. And then you'll be able to think better."

Skye wriggled deeper under her covers. "Can't I just—"

"No, you cannot," Gran said, springing to her feet in a surprisingly youthful way. "Up, up, up!"

"So, you can come over tomorrow afternoon at three?" Skye asked Maddy over the phone that evening—lucky, innocent Maddy, who hadn't been at the dance the night before. Maddy was the last kid on Skye's list of people to call. "Amanda's coming, and so are Pip and Matteo and Jamila."

"I guess," Maddy said, sounding reluctant. "I was going to watch a rerun of the meerkat show at four P.M., though. Can we watch it at your house?"

"If there's time," Skye assured her. *If you're still talking to me by then,* she added silently.

"And it's a party, right?" Maddy asked, cheering up.

"It's *like* a party," Skye told her. "I really need you to be here, Maddy."

"Okay," Maddy said. "If you need me, I'll be there— because you're my best friend, Skye, and I would never let you down."

20

Something Like Okay

"**R**ise and shine, Skye," Gran said on Sunday morning, repeating the previous morning's gentle command.

"But I was up really late last night, planning what I'm gonna say to my friends," Skye mumbled from underneath her covers. "I even wrote it all out, like a script."

"Well, should I tell him to leave?" Gran asked in a brisk, cheerful voice.

Him?

Skye sat bolt upright in bed, her heart pounding. "Who's here?" she asked.

"You'll see," Gran said—and she was smiling.

"So here it is," Kee Matthews said ten minutes later in Gran's living room as he handed Skye her sketchbook, which was complete, except for the few drawings that had been taped to the gymnasium wall on Friday night. "Not that Aaron probably even knows yet that I swiped it back from him," he added.

Um, okay, obviously I am wishing that I'd worn something cuter. And brushed my hair.

"He's going to be so mad," Skye said, admiring Kee's courage. "But he should never have taken it in the first place."

"Well, you shouldn't have made us look so dumb in that Homecoming newspaper, either," Kee said, frowning. "It was a really big deal."

"I know," Skye admitted softly.

"And you, like, totally ruined everything," Kee continued, relentless. "Aaron says that's why he dropped the ball in the fourth quarter."

Even angry he was cute, Skye thought, in spite of herself. "I'm sorry," she told him. "But you guys were being so—"

"I know, I know," Kee interrupted, obviously embarrassed.

"Well, but how come you hang out with them, then?" Skye asked.

Kee shrugged one narrow shoulder. "I dunno," he

admitted. "I might have to rethink that, now—whether I want to or not. But you gotta hang with someone, don't you? And they can be okay—when there aren't any girls around, anyway. We have fun."

"But what about Aaron picking on Pip all the time?" Skye argued. "Pip's not a girl, he's another guy. And he's an *artist*. He's pretty good, in fact. And you, of all people, should understand about that."

"Why me of all people?" Kee asked, frowning.

DANKO, Prince of Darkness??

"'Cause you're an artist, too," Skye said shyly. "I like those drawings you gave me, Kee."

"What drawings?" Kee asked, a look of total incomprehension on his face. "Oh," he said suddenly, and he smiled.

"What?" Skye asked. "Who did them, if it wasn't you?"

"Danko," Kee said, stunning Skye with the one word. "It had to be him."

"*Who?*"

"You heard me," Kee said. "It had to be Danko. He kind of likes you, see, and he loves to draw, only hardly anybody knows it. But I told him a few weeks ago about how you were secretly drawing everyone. After I saw you that time on the steps," Kee reminded her.

"But—but—but how come Danko's not taking art, if he likes it so much?" Skye asked, sputtering. "And—he *likes* me? And how come he just goes along with Aaron and Cord when they call Pip names and everything? "

"Maybe he doesn't like Pip, I dunno," Kee said, shrugging. "You can't like everyone. Or maybe it's because of Danko's brothers. His dad, too, 'cause his dad's a real hard-nose about stuff like guys taking art. All Mr. Marshall cares about is sports, and now Danko can't even show him the Homecoming newspaper when he gets home from his business trip, thanks to you. And that was, like, his *only thing.*"

Skye wasn't exactly sure what a hard-nose was, though she had a pretty good idea. "But you swiped my sketchbook back," she said slowly. "Why?"

Kee shrugged again, then looked away. "I felt sorry for you, I guess," he said quietly. "With your brother so messed up and everything. Also, I didn't want them to ruin any of your drawings. Not that Aaron's exactly going to understand my thinking."

"Well, thanks," Skye said, wishing she could stop the blush that was spreading up her neck and across her face. "But you don't have to feel sorry for me, Kee, 'cause my brother's—"

"He's gonna be okay?" Kee asked, sounding hopeful.

"I don't know," Skye admitted, her voice soft. "He'll be something like okay, I think. Eventually. But—I'd do it again, you know," she told him suddenly. "If I had to."

"Do what?"

"Fight back," Skye said. "'Specially if Aaron or Cord ever, ever touch Maddy again, or if Melissa and Taylor don't start laying off Amanda and the rest of us girls. I've got some pretty good drawings of them I could use, you know."

"I know," Kee said, smiling a little. "They saw them. We all saw them."

"And I could always make more," Skye said, feeling a little foolish, but glad to have said what she did.

"Tough guy," Kee teased.

"Excuse me, you two," Gran said, poking her head into the living room. "But would you like some delicious soda and chips? Even though it's still morning?"

Uh, thanks?

Okay, I can't help it.
He's a little bit my hero.
(For the moment, anyway.)

I love you, Skye thought, touched by Gran's struggle to please her.

"Sure," Kee said, obviously relieved at the interruption.

"I'll be right back," Gran said, beaming, and she disappeared into the kitchen to get their snack.

"You're gonna *really* feel sorry for me when you taste those chips," Skye whispered, daring a smile.

"Huh?" Kee said.

"You'll find out," Skye told him.

21

Real, True Friends

Now that she had her sketchbook back, Skye wanted to cancel the afternoon get-together—but Gran wouldn't hear of it. "Out of the question, Skye," she said firmly. "You cannot un-invite your friends to a party at the last minute, short of being abducted by aliens," she added, pausing to inspect a carrot she'd been peeling for the vegetable platter that was to be the star of the snack table.

"But this wasn't even supposed to *be* a party," Skye pointed out. "It was supposed to be kind of like a meeting. You know, just so I could warn everyone about the rest of the drawings in my sketchbook. I was afraid they'd end up plastered all over the walls at school, at the very least. But everything's okay now, Gran."

"One more hour," Gran said, glancing at her watch.

"But—but I'm still too new in Sierra Madre to give a party," Skye objected.

"You're too new to have friends?" Gran asked, cocking her curly brown head in inquiry. "Because if those five kids who jumped at the chance to come over this afternoon aren't friends, then what are they?"

"They didn't exactly *jump*," Skye argued feebly. "Not all of them, anyway. I had to promise Maddy that she wouldn't miss some TV show about meerkats. But—"

"But nothing," Gran said briskly, expertly chopping the carrot into neat sticks. "As I recall, you didn't have to argue with any one of them. And even though this sketchbook situation isn't going to get any worse, I think you still owe those kids an explanation about the drawings you did of them that got put up at the dance."

"I guess," Skye mumbled.

"Maybe you even owe your friends an apology," Gran suggested.

"They aren't officially my friends," Skye objected, hearing how lame her objection sounded even as she stated it. "And I never meant for anyone to see *any* of the drawings," she added, defending herself—and practicing a little for the speech she'd apparently still have to give that afternoon. "Not to mention that Maddy and Jamila weren't even *at* the dance," she pointed out. "So won't I just be stirring up trouble if I tell them—"

"You know Maddy and Jamila will hear about it eventually," Gran interrupted. "And those kids are your new friends, Skye, whether you want to admit it or not. I thought you were getting used to living with me here in Sierra Madre, sweetheart," she added, her voice softening. "I hoped you were, anyway. I certainly love having you here."

"I *am* getting used to it," Skye mumbled. "*Too* used to it, maybe! Because this is only temporary, and sooner or later, I have to go back."

It wasn't *"back home"* anymore, Skye noted, surprised—just *"back."*

"Not necessarily," Gran said carefully, turning to wash a green pepper under cool running water. "This whole situation isn't only about Scotty, Skye. Everyone—including your mom and your dad—wants what's best for you. We want you never to feel trapped. And you do have a say in the matter."

"Really?" Skye asked.

"Really."

"Well, one thing I have to say," Skye said suddenly, "is that I wouldn't put that green pepper on the platter if I were you, Gran—or Maddy will *freak*, and that's all we need to make it a perfect afternoon."

"Oh, my gosh, you're right!" Gran said, smacking her head with the plump palm of her hand. "Now, that *would* have been a disaster."

"A little one, anyway," Skye said, laughing.

"And we've had enough of the other kind, haven't we?" Gran said, reeling Skye in for a hug.

"And so I just wanted to say that I'm sorry if anyone was embarrassed Friday night by those drawings, or if your feelings got hurt," Skye told Amanda, Matteo, Jamila, Pip, and a confused-looking Maddy an hour later. "I didn't mean anything bad when I did them, and anyway, they were supposed to be private."

Amanda scowled. "But I don't get it," she said. "Why did you even draw us that way? I thought you liked us! And you made me look like a—"

"I do like you," Skye interrupted hastily. "I mostly drew those pictures when I first got here, and I didn't even know you guys. Not really. And I was feeling really bad about—about *everything*, so I kind of took it out on you. You're not the only one with a dark inner life, you know," she told Amanda, hoping she would remember the time she'd proudly claimed that for herself.

"Sorry about your brother," Pip mumbled, looking embarrassed.

"Yeah," Matteo said, eyeing the bowl of chips. "That's gotta suck."

"Scott's better than he was last summer," Skye assured them. "And it's funny," she continued, "but he and I are a lot closer since I've been living far away. Closer than we've been since we were little kids."

"Well, that's good, I guess," Jamila said. "But getting back to those drawings—what did the one of me look like?"

"You looked good, naturally," Amanda said, sounding a little bitter. "But Skye made *me* look like a—"

"I'm sorry," Skye said again. She looked at Maddy, to include her in the apology, but Maddy was staring down at Gran's rug as if she were inspecting it for dust mites.

"So where are they?" Jamila interrupted, looking around the living room.

"They got thrown out," Skye told her, mourning her lost drawings only a little. "By one of the committee moms."

"This isn't over, though," Pip said, frowning. "Because those guys still have your sketchbook."

"But they don't," Skye told everyone eagerly. "I got it back! Someone gave it to me this morning."

"Who?" Jamila asked. "One of the grown-ups at the dance?"

"Who cares who it was?" Matteo said, helping himself

to a handful of chips. "This whole thing *is* over, if you've got the sketchbook back. So let's eat!"

"Maddy?" Skye asked quietly, as the other kids swarmed over Gran's assorted snacks and jabbered excitedly about Friday night. "Are we okay?"

"I feel fine, thank you," Maddy said, misunderstanding Skye's question.

"Then why won't you look at me?" Skye asked.

"Because I don't want to," Maddy said, still studying the rug. "You made a joke out of me in front of everyone, and I thought you were my real, true friend."

"I didn't make a joke out of you," Skye tried to explain. "I drew a cartoon of you when I moved here last summer, before I even really got to know you. I drew crazy pictures of *everyone*, Maddy! I never meant for anyone else to see them, though."

"But I don't get it," Maddy said, frowning in concentration. "How is a mean picture supposed to be funny? I would never do something like that to you, Skye."

"Maybe you're nicer than I am," Skye replied, meaning every word. "And anyway," she continued, "the pictures I drew were just supposed to be funny to *me*. My sketchbook was like my diary, Maddy. But I'm very, very sorry if I hurt your feelings. I just—like I said before, I was feeling really bad when I had to move here."

"Feeling bad from keeping so many secrets?" Maddy asked, finally looking at Skye. "Like about having a brother, and about being an artist?"

"I guess," Skye said. "I kind of liked having a few secrets," she added, surprised by her own admission. "But that's private, okay? Just between you and me."

"*Another* secret?" a startled Maddy asked.

"But this is the good kind," Skye assured her. "It's the kind of secret friends share."

"Because we *are* friends, right?" Maddy asked, obviously trying to get things straight. "Real, true friends? If I forgive you?"

"Mm-hmm," Skye said, nodding.

Maddy thought—for what seemed to Skye like a long, long time. "Then I forgive you, Skye," she finally said. "Because anyone can make a mistake. But I'm probably missing the meerkats this very minute, so maybe I'd better go home."

"I'll ask Gran to turn on the TV, okay?" Skye said. "That way, you can watch the meerkats here, Maddy. Because I really want you to stay."

"Okay," Maddy said, smiling. "Go ask!"

22

Big, Big Trouble

HI SKYE! YOU WILL BE HERE THS WEDSDAY, BUT THER IS
A SUPRISE! WE ARE GONG TO SANTA FE FOR THNSKGVNG
AND SPND 3 DAYS, ITS A PRESNT FRM GRAN. WE STAYE IN
A HOTL, MOM SAYS WE EVEN GET RM SEVICE IF WE WANT
2! NO MATTR WHAT HAPPNS WITH MOM AND DAD, YOU
AND I HAV FUN, OK? ALWASE. I MISS YOU! LOVE, SCOTT

Dear Scott, Really? That is so cool about Santa Fe!! But I
still have to go to school for 2 1/2 more days. Be thinking of
me after lunch today, okay? Because I have a feeling I am in
big, big trouble with my art teacher.
Love, Skye
P.S. I got my sketchbook back! I'll tell you all about it
when I see you. Oh, and some of my friends came over

this afternoon. I thought it was going to be terrible, but we ended up having a lot of fun. Gran even sent out for 3 pizzas, one plain cheese pizza just for Maddy!

@

"Front and center, art activities kids," a grim-looking Ms. O'Hare said a few minutes after art class began on Monday and the students had gotten to work on their torn paper collages. "Gather around my desk, if you please."

Skye, Amanda, Jamila, Matteo, and Pip shot each other brief, panicky glances, then sidled up to their teacher's desk. Ms. O'Hare pulled a cardboard file out of her gingham-lined tote, opened it, and placed the Homecoming newspaper insert square on her desk. "So," she said, and then she waited, as if the other kids in class—industriously snipping and gluing, and pretending not to listen—didn't know exactly what was happening.

Silent, Skye and the other art activities kids stared down at the insert as if hypnotized; Skye's four drawings seemed to jump off the page.

"We'll gather after school for a short meeting, people," Ms. O'Hare told them. "No excuses. And that includes Maddy, Skye. You can round her up."

"But I have gymnastics," Matteo argued feebly.

"And I have track," Jamila chimed in.

"After school, and no excuses," Ms. O'Hare said again,

sounding more like a scary principal than an art teacher, in Skye's opinion. "This was a group effort, and you'll face the consequences as a group."

I never saw an art teacher this mad before.

"You really let me down," Ms. O'Hare said when everyone assembled after classes had ended for the day—everyone, including the still-grumbling Matteo and Jamila and Maddy, who, though terror-stricken, had quietly told Skye she would share the blame, if that would help.

"That's what friends are for," Maddy solemnly said.

"This—this *escapade* really makes me look bad, do you realize that?" Ms. O'Hare told her art activities kids. "It makes it seem as though I don't know what's going on in my own class! And the art department is on thin ice around here already."

The art activities kids shifted back and forth, scared that one of them was going to say something about what they'd done, or about why they wanted to get revenge—or

What have we done?
Maybe we should have thought this through a little better...

that no one would say anything. Skye didn't know which would be worse.

"Now, I know whose drawings these are," Ms. O'Hare continued gravely. "I recognize the line. But I'd like that person to step forward and take full responsibility."

Jamila scowled. "I wasn't even at the dance, so it's not me," she objected, though that wouldn't clear her at all if she were the guilty one, Skye thought, working it out.

"I was at the dance," Amanda admitted. "But I didn't have any fun, if that counts."

Frozen where she stood, Skye suddenly heard the sound of her beating heart echo in her ears. Did this mean she was about to faint? She cleared her throat. "I—"

"It was all of us," Pip interrupted, his voice surprisingly firm. "Even Jamila and Amanda. We all thought up the idea. We just talked Skye into doing the drawings, that's all. She didn't know any better, 'cause she's new here. She's like a foreign-exchange student, practically."

"I am not," Skye objected hotly. "I'm from New Mexico, in the U.S.A. It's just two states over! *Geez.*"

"It was our forty-seventh state," loyal Maddy confirmed. "And it has been, ever since 1912."

"What on earth made you do such a thing, Skye?" Ms. O'Hare asked her, ignoring the history lesson.

A dozen thoughts chased each other around inside Skye's head, because—how could she explain? That she was getting even with those football guys for "colliding" with Maddy that first day, for trying to hurt Amanda's feelings, and for kicking Pip? Or that she was getting even with Melissa and Taylor, too, for all their snotty comments? And that she wanted to get even with any mean person in the future who might tease or torment Maddy or Scott—or anyone else with anything wrong with them?

That, in a weird way, she was trying to make Sierra Madre seem more real?

None of it sounded very plausible, even if all of it was the truth.

"You ruined a souvenir of a very special day in those boys' lives," Ms. O'Hare said. "Also, you abused both your talent and the trust I placed in you all to do a professional job on this paper. And now, we have to figure out a way of making things right for those four boys. First, an apology is in order."

"We're sorry," the art kids mumbled in unison.

"Don't apologize to *me*, for heaven's sake," Ms. O'Hare said, shaking her head in exasperation. "Apologize to the boys you wronged! And here they are now."

And, to the horror of Skye and all the other art activities kids, Aaron Petterson, Danko Marshall, Cord Driscoll, and Kee Williams came slinking into the room, accompanied by their football coach. Kee looked briefly at Skye and gave her a secret smile so small that his mouth barely moved, and Danko glanced at her once, then blushed and looked away.

And for the first time in weeks, Skye wished again that she were invisible—just so she could stare deep into Danko's eyes and search for the artist who was hiding somewhere inside.

She wanted to know what he'd been trying to say.

23

Making Things Right

"**A**pologize to these nice young men," Ms. O'Hare instructed her wayward little flock.

"We're sorry," most of the art kids chorused, fingers crossed behind one or two backs.

Pip, however, had something else to say. "They aren't nice, and we only did what we did because we had to," he said loudly, his voice shaking a little.

"Why did you have to?" Ms. O'Hare asked, frowning.

"Because those boys kept calling Pip against-the-law names, that's why," Amanda said, stepping forward, her voice squeaking more than ever. "Like '*pansy*' and—" She whispered the bad words to Ms. O'Hare. "Especially Aaron and Cord! And Melissa and Taylor. And they aren't so nice to me, either."

"They're mean," Matteo and Jamila confirmed, heads nodding.

"And I know it's not a good thing to tattle," Maddy said, after raising her hand, "but sometimes Aaron and Cord bump into me on purpose, and they call me '*retard.*' And those two girls do it, also."

Skye knew how much courage it had taken Maddy to speak up, and she gave her friend's cold hand a warm squeeze.

Coach turned to face his players. "Is any of this true?" he asked quietly.

"No," a sullen Aaron replied.

"They're lying," Cord said.

"*All* of them?" Coach asked, folding his big arms across his chest.

"They aren't lying," Kee said, stepping forward. "I guess we should apologize or something. All of us."

"Yeah, maybe," Danko mumbled.

"At the very least," Coach said. "This sounds pretty serious, if you ask me."

And they didn't know the worst of it, Skye thought, remembering when Pip had been shoved and kicked around just before Halloween. But that was their secret, she and Pip had decided.

"It sounds *very* serious," a troubled-looking Ms. O'Hare

replied. "You kids should have spoken up earlier," she added, turning to her students.

"But it didn't happen in class," Skye tried to explain. "And Melissa and Taylor aren't even here. They'll never get in trouble, no matter what! They're not the type."

"We'll take care of them later, if this information is accurate," Ms. O'Hare assured her students. "But you must speak up to an adult when bad things happen."

"Okay," everyone mumbled with varying degrees of sincerity.

"Aaron and Cord, apologize to these young artists," Coach said.

Cord's eyes narrowed, but he didn't dare disobey. "I'm sorry," he mumbled.

"Me, too," Aaron said, looking away.

"Say it, Aaron," Coach told him. "And look them in the eyes like a man."

"I *apologize*," Aaron said, almost spitting out the words.

"I'll take care of some of this on the playing field," Coach said, glaring at all four of his players. "Some extra push-ups and laps will help remind the team how athletes should behave, and I'm sure the

guys will be grateful to Aaron and Cord for the reminder. But the entire school should talk more about this—this *bullying* problem after Thanksgiving break, so I think Ms. O'Hare and I will take it to the principal, and we'll talk about doing some school-wide sensitivity training."

Horrified, all the kids tried to stifle their groans.

"I agree," Ms. O'Hare said, nodding her head. "And for the art activities kids' part, making things right is important, so my students are all going to chip in to reprint the inserts for the four of you *this very week* on the best paper money can buy," Ms. O'Hare told the football players. "So they can sign them for all the other students, as planned, and so they'll be able to show them to their grandchildren someday."

Skye almost lost it at that point, thinking of any of those boys being somebody's grandfather, but she stared at the ground and stifled her nervous giggles.

"So, will that do it, Coach?" Ms. O'Hare asked the football coach, who had just stolen a glance at his watch.

"I believe so," he said, nodding solemnly. "But do you

have the original drawings handy? Because a couple of the boys wanted to keep theirs."

"*Really?*" Ms. O'Hare asked, astonished.

"Really," the coach confirmed. "And I'd love it if whoever did them would draw a nice one of me, too, after we get back from break. If it's not too much trouble, that is. I'd love to frame it and give it to Mrs. Coach for Christmas."

Mrs. Coach! Skye was delighted, hearing him call his wife that, and when she looked up, to her astonishment, Danko was grinning, too—but he wiped the smile off his face almost instantly, and he resumed his habitual blank, sullen stare.

The art activities kids all looked at Skye. "Sure," she said, croaking out the word. "I'll be happy to draw a picture of you, Mr., um, Coach. And the originals are right over there," she added, pointing to the teetering pile of papers left over from the Homecoming newspaper project. "I'll just go get them."

"And then we can all go home," Ms. O'Hare said. "Because I, for one, am in absolute *shreds.*"

⑥

Dear Scott, Well, I'll be home in just one more day! It's too bad Gran is staying in Sierra Madre for the holiday, but at least she will be celebrating with her (maybe invisible) boyfriend.

I did get in trouble Monday, in fact all the art jerks did. But the hardest thing was for me to apologize privately to Ms. O'Hare, which I did because I like her, she trusted me, and I blew it. But she forgave me, because nobody's perfect, right?

Love, Skye

(P.S. You are my keyboarding assignment today. . . .)

SANTA FE

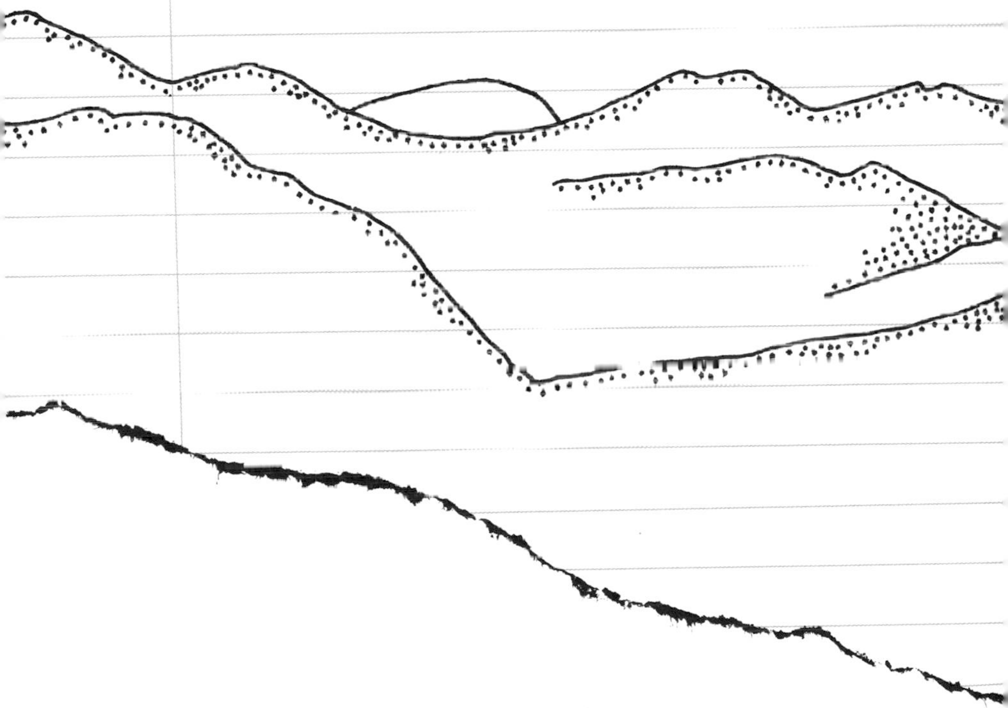

24

Family Reunion

"**N**eed to stop?" the Albuquerque airline representative asked, pausing by a restroom.

"No thanks," Skye told her, embarrassed both by the question and by having to be accompanied at all, though it was the rule until she was fifteen. "I'm fine."

"Okay, but stick close," the woman called out, clacking across the brown tiled floor again with leggy strides. "I don't want to lose you in this crowd."

"You won't," Skye shouted, hurrying to keep up. The Albuquerque International Sunport was jammed today with people—edgy parents, scared or excited little kids— intent upon their holiday travels, and Skye was momentarily homesick for Gran, and Sierra Madre.

"I hope someone's waiting," the woman said, sounding irritated in advance over the possibility of some glitch. "Because they'll have to sign off on you."

"Someone will be there," Skye promised, hoping it was true. The woman was making her sound like an unwanted parcel, which Skye hoped she was not.

But the truth was, she didn't know *what* to expect this Thanksgiving, because—was everything going to be okay with her mom, her dad, and Scott? Or "something *like* okay," the way she had put it to Kee last Sunday morning?

Skye actually felt nervous about her own family reunion.

She spotted them at once, in spite of the many people pushing toward the baggage carousel like iron filings being drawn to a giant horseshoe magnet. Scott was sitting on a brown leather bench, probably trying to look as if nothing was wrong with him, though his walker—complete with yellow tennis balls on its front legs—crouched nearby. Her mom leaned against a square pillar, while a few feet away, her dad scanned bobbing heads in the crowd like a human radar device.

Her mom looked old, Skye thought, feeling guilty about sounding so critical—or if not old, old*er*. Her hair needed cutting, and she'd gotten thinner, and she wasn't wearing any lipstick.

"Skye!" her father shouted, waving his arms in the air. "There's our girl," he announced to his wife and Scott.

"*Darling*," her mother said, rushing over to greet Skye with a warm embrace.

Her mom still smelled the same, Skye thought gratefully—like lemonade, or something else sweet and citrus-y. She had missed her mother's hugs. "I'm here," Skye announced unnecessarily.

Darling!

"Oh, *you*," Mrs. McPhee said quietly, giving Skye another squeeze.

I didn't realize how much I missed Mom 'til I saw her again!

"Hi, Mom," Skye said, her voice muffled against her mother's dress. "This lady says you guys are supposed to sign something saying I got here okay."

"I'll take care of that," Skye's dad said, smiling broadly at the toe-tapping airline representative as he scribbled his name. "You have a nice Thanksgiving, now," he called out to her disappearing back.

"We're heading straight up to Santa Fe so we won't waste a moment of our vacation," her mom told Skye, sounding excited. "Oh, and here comes Scott!"

Scott looked a bit fatter, Skye thought as her brother laboriously approached with his walker. It was as though he'd gained all the weight their mom had lost. But compared to last August, anyway, he seemed to be moving around a lot better. "Hey," she greeted him, feeling strangely shy. She leaned over the front of Scott's walker to give him an awkward hug.

"Hey, Skye," Scott said back. "*Art jerk*," he whispered, grinning.

This new Scott is different, but so am I.

"What does your bag look like, Skye?" her dad asked, scanning the carousel.

"It's that old green duffel," Skye reminded him. "And Gran put a big orange X on the side of it with tape."

"Sounds familiar," her dad said with a smile. "It should be here pretty soon." He turned to his wife. "Why don't you and Scotty go get the van, and then meet us at the loading zone?" he suggested. "That'll be his physical therapy for the day."

For a moment, it looked as though Scott was going to argue, but—in the spirit of their upcoming mini-vacation, a relieved Skye supposed—he just shrugged, then headed toward the wide glass door that led outside, his mother trailing after him.

Her dad looked tired, Skye thought anxiously as she stole a peek at him. "So, how's Scott really doing?" she asked, feeling a little disloyal to her brother—her newest friend, in a strange way—for talking about him behind his back. But she had to know.

Her dad sighed as the same few orphaned suitcases cruised around once more. "He's doing a lot better, honey," he said. "The seizures have pretty much stopped, and he's not as depressed as he was, and he's cooperating with his rehab people more. I guess the meds are working."

Meds. Becoming familiar with a term like that was never a good sign, Skye thought sadly.

"It was real sweet of you to answer all those e-mails of his," her dad was saying, distracted now by the new bags that had started to hurtle down the chute toward the carousel. "One of his therapists was just saying how much his small motor skills have improved, at least in part because of all that keyboarding."

How patronizing, Skye thought, scowling. "Well, thanks," she mumbled. "But I wasn't being sweet, Dad—except at first, maybe. But after that, I *wanted* him to write me, and I liked writing him back."

So there, she added silently.

"Don't worry, we'll be chowing down on chiles rellenos and sopapillas before you know it, Skye," her father said, glancing at the expression on her face and mistaking it for hunger. "You're back in New Mexico. Welcome home, honey!"

25

This New Scott

~~~

"So, you got busted, huh?" Scott asked quietly in the backseat of the McPhees' new van, after removing his ear-buds and clearing his throat. He actually looked as shy as Skye had felt about forty minutes earlier, she noted, surprised.

Skye's parents sat without speaking in the front of the van—as if there were an invisible wall between them.

"Busted big-time," Skye whispered, trying to smile. "And it's gonna get worse when I get back," she added, thinking of the threatened sensitivity meeting.

But at least that meeting would probably keep Aaron, Cord, and the bad ballerinas in line for the immediate future—not because of anything amazing the principal might say, but because of those kids' fear of further incurring the wrath of the entire meeting-hating student body.

"Tell me about it later," Scott mouthed, jerking his head toward the front seat.

"Okay," Skye whispered back, and she resumed staring out of the boxy van's windows at the gray-bottomed clouds above their car, clouds that streaked the surrounding landscape with shadow.

The McPhees were well on their way north to Santa Fe, about an hour's drive in all. Albuquerque's looming Sandia Peaks—bare, brown, dusted with snow at the top, and wrapped with cloud shadows—had slipped behind them. Ahead, the distant snowy peaks behind Santa Fe and Taos—which lay even farther north than the McPhees' destination—seemed to beckon.

Interstate 25 shot straight through the desert, climbing gradually as it passed a small town—Bernalillo—and several pueblos that were invisible from the highway. Wild winter-gold grass sprawled for miles in every direction, Skye noted, its expanse punctuated only by the dark green bushes that looked like shaggy marbles someone had flung across the desert floor.

Skye sighed. The truth was, she was feeling weirdly awkward around this new Scott, because—who was he, now? Obviously, her brother was not the pint-sized hero who'd towed her around the neighborhood in his Radio Flyer when they were little. And he wasn't the moody whirlwind who'd basically dominated their lives for the past four years. And he wasn't, thank goodness, the cursing, raving Scott of last summer.

This new Scott, the Scott who had been e-mailing her for the past three months, seemed unfamiliar to Skye—as if, in the nine months that had passed since his accident, an entirely new person had been born.

This Scott—in his e-mails, anyway—could be angry and self-pitying, true. So could she. But he could also be funny, brave, and even optimistic, in spite of everything.

And he truly cared about her once more. They cared about each other.

But where had this new Scott McPhee been for the past four years, Skye wondered? Hidden, like the artist inside Danko Marshall?

And why had it taken a tragedy for that person to emerge?

It didn't seem to Skye as if their van had driven uphill at all, but it had; they were now only a few miles south of Santa Fe. There were puzzle pieces of snow by the road now, and many more bushes on the surrounding slopes.

It occurred suddenly to a half-awake Skye that there was so much horizon in this part of New Mexico—spreading for miles in a complete circle around her family's car—

that they must be somewhere near the exact center of the universe, or at least at the heart of the world. "X marks the spot," she whispered sleepily.

"Huh?" Scott asked, removing his ear-buds once more.

"Tell you later," Skye said, echoing her brother's earlier words.

26

forever

~~~

"No leftovers. That's the only bad thing about Thanksgiving in a hotel," Skye said late Friday morning, the day after Thanksgiving, as she and Scott sat bundled up on a bench in chilly sunlight in Santa Fe's central plaza. Behind them, skeletal trees cast lacy shadows on the remains of the snow—dirt-sifted now—that had fallen a week earlier.

Skye had dreamed about Christmas in Santa Fe the night before, she suddenly remembered, surprised that her imagination had picked the wrong holiday to celebrate. It had been a lavender-blue twilight in her dream, and very cold, with snow decorating the tops of the town's adobe walls like white frosting on flat-roofed gingerbread houses, and she was all alone. But hundreds of *farolitos* lined every walkway and rooftop, and they warmed her with their glow.

Farolitos were simple lanterns made with small white candles placed in sand-weighted brown paper bags, or— more recently—electric lights inside plastic "paper bags," and they were a real New Mexico thing, especially in the winter. Skye's dad had told her once that the word *"faro-litos"* meant "little lighthouses," because that's what the finished lanterns kind of looked like. And that comparison had been perfect for her dream—because somehow, she just knew that those little lighthouses were guiding her. They were keeping her safe.

She'd been lost in her dream, but because of the *faroli-tos*, she had not been afraid as she wandered through the deserted town.

And in her dream, Skye could hear the floating, in-and-out sound of people chanting and singing as she walked the empty streets, and the heartbeat of distant drums, and even though she couldn't find those people no matter which corner she turned, she knew they were nearby. She wasn't alone.

It had been so cool.

"Putting green chiles in the stuffing," Scott reminded her in the new, painstaking way of speaking he had that made it sound as if the words were crawling into and out of his head one at a time. "*That's* the bad thing about Thanksgiving in a hotel."

"They put green chiles in everything in this town," Skye observed as she tried to sketch the sticking-up monument in the middle of the plaza. "But other people's stuffing always tastes wrong, in my opinion."

Scott sighed and looked at his watch. "How long are Mom and Dad gonna be gone?" he asked.

"At least until three," Skye said, shifting her bottom on the uneven wooden slats and leaning back against the ornate bench's cold, green metal sculptural flourishes. "It's supposed to be like a date for them, remember? The folk art museum, and then their own private romantic lunch. But we've got money for lunch, too—just as soon as I finish my drawing."

"It's not gonna work," Scott said gloomily.

"Well, I don't have a ruler," Skye said, eyeing the tall, skinny monument with a frown.

"I meant their date," Scott told her. "They'll still argue. They've always argued."

Skye was silent for a couple of minutes as she drew. Scott was right, their parents *had* always argued, even before the accident. It seemed important to Skye that she remember this. "But we're us, not them," she reminded her brother.

"I gotta move around, or my legs won't work," Scott told Skye. "It's freezing."

"Well, so move around, then," Skye told him, because — did they have to do absolutely everything together? "Do a couple of laps around the plaza, and by then I'll be done," she told him, softening her tone.

"I don't know," Scott said reluctantly, scanning the crowded area.

Wherever she and Scott went, Skye had observed in the past two days, a weird sort of vacuum seemed to be created behind them as they walked, a vacuum that caused strangers' heads to turn as they nervously wondered what calamity had happened that had placed a sixteen-year-old kid behind a walker. Once, some little kids had mimicked him behind his back, and Skye wanted to scream at them.

That head-turning and mimicking would probably

I guess they don't know any better,
but WHO CARES?
They're still yucky little twerps.

happen in California, too, Skye thought—if the McPhees really moved there.

Scott stood up a little unsteadily and reached for his walker. "They'll still fight in Sierra Madre," he told Skye, big brother to little sister.

"I know that," she replied, not looking up from her drawing. "Moving wouldn't fix everything. But they think it would be a fresh start for everyone." *Mostly you, Scott,* she added silently. "Dad might not even be able to get a job in Southern California," Skye reminded her brother. "Or that tenant in Gran's rental unit might decide not to move out after all," she added, trying not to think that far ahead, because—what was the point, when anything at all might happen to any one of them?

Skye had learned that the hard way.

But good things could happen, too. Just look at the friends she'd made and the adventures she'd had in all-too-real Sierra Madre!

She would always, always have to come up with her own plan, Skye decided as she drew, and then hope for the best. And as of right now, her plan was to stay in Sierra Madre with Gran until the end of the school year, at the very least, if she was allowed to. Or maybe even longer. And always to keep writing to—and loving—her brother.

Loving him forever.

☆❀MY BROTHER and ME❀☆
FROM NOW ON

1. I am separate from my Mom + Dad and their ≈PROBLEMS.≈
2. I am also separate from SCOTT.
3. But I love Scott and he loves me.
4. I will always do what I can to help him.
5. I get to decide what that is, though!

"But there's good doctors in California, right?" Scott asked, shuffling his legs back and forth in an attempt to warm them up. "Right, Skye? Good doctors? In case we really do get to move?"

"That's right, Scotty," Skye said, closing her sketchbook with a sigh. "They have really good doctors in California." She got to her feet.

"Then I'm ready to move there," Scott said quietly. "It'll be easier, 'cause this is me, now, Skye—only no one knows that in Albuquerque. In California, new kids can just like it or lump it when they meet me, instead of comparing me to my old self. Let's go," he said, changing the subject. "Where d'you want to eat?"

"Somewhere close," Skye told him, not knowing what else to say. "Only I want to stop by the library so I can check my e-mail."

"You still think Hana will write?" Scott asked, teasing her.

Skye whirled to face him. "No fair using the private stuff we wrote each other against me," she said.

"Not in real life," Scott agreed, as hastily as he could. "Sorry, Skye."

"And maybe *Maddy* wrote me, did you ever think of that?" Skye said, her voice still quavering as she thought about the girl who had taught her so much about loyalty—

and even bravery. "She's my friend now, too. Or maybe Amanda e-mailed me, or Pip, or maybe even Kee! Or maybe Hana *did* e-mail me, even though she hates writing," she added. "But Hana probably wouldn't write a ransom note if she were kidnapped, so it's not exactly like my feelings are gonna be hurt even if she *never* writes. We were still friends, though. That was real."

"I think it's usually the bad guy who writes the ransom note," Scott said cautiously as they began their step-*bump*, step-*bump*, step-*bump* way across one of the plaza's diagonal paths.

Maybe friends are friends forever, if you keep them in your heart. (That's how I feel about Hana, anyway.)

"You know what I mean about private, Scott," she insisted. "That's how it has to be, if we're going to be stick together."

"Yeah, I know," Scott said. "But I think Hana is still your friend," he added shyly. "Anyone would want to be your friend, Skye."

"Huh," she said, feeling shy as well, but pleased.

Her big brother's awkward words were comforting to Skye, and she warmed herself with them as morning ended and she and Scott made their way across the ancient plaza, through the clear, cold light.

Acknowledgments

First, I acknowledge my indebtedness to Pasadena's former Neurological Learning Center, where some time ago I worked for a year with brain-injured young adults, assisting the art therapist and, later, teaching drawing. My time there left me with an awareness both of the devastating effects of these all-too-common injuries and of the hope that endures in the young people who suffer such injuries. I came away from that time with enormous sympathy and respect for that center's clients and their families. I hope those sentiments are reflected in this work.

Next, I give sincere thanks to three people at Curtis Brown, Ltd.: my agent Ginger Knowlton, her assistant Tracy Marchini, and foreign-rights agent Dave Barbor. I am grateful to all three for their invaluable support. I also once again thank Tracy Gates, my longtime editor at Viking Children's Books. I value her taste, humor, empathy, stamina—and her willingness to listen to my occasionally off-the-wall ideas. It is always a productive pleasure working with her. In addition, I thank Viking's art department, especially Nancy Brennan and Sam Kim for all their hard work on this challenging project.

Additionally, I thank Pasadena artist and musician Alex Twomey for creating the three "mystery drawings" for this book. I also thank a friend I've known since the day he was born, glassblower and future writer Evan Chambers, who shared the plan for his inspired Halloween costume with me and invited me to use it in this book.

Finally, I thank my great friend Debby Schwartz for her fierce and uncritical loyalty. I need it! And, always, I thank my husband, the writer Christopher Davis, for his unwavering support and for his open-hearted willingness to adopt and listen to my many chattering characters long enough for me to get the job done.